"Look out!" screamed Calamity.

Even as Choya fired and almost before Calamity screamed her warning, the young Texan acted. Three times he fired, working the lever in almost a blur of movement. Choya got off one shot which fanned the Texan's cheek in passing and might have hit if the *Comanchero's* hand had been steadier. Twice splinters erupted from the wall, drawing closer to Choya. On the third shot no splinters flew, but the *Comanchero* jerked under the impact of lead. For an instant he struggled to keep his gun lined.

The Texan levered another bullet into his rifle and prepared to shoot again. The precaution proved to be unnecessary. Opening his hand, Choya let the Remington fall.

This time, when the gun landed on the ground, Choya would not be picking it up again.

Books by J.T. Edson

RUNNING IRONS
WACO'S BADGE
TEXAS KILLERS
COLD DECK, HOT LEAD

J.T.
EDSON

RUNNING
IRONS

HarperTorch
An Imprint of HarperCollins*Publishers*

This is a work of fiction. Names, characters, places, and incidents are products of the author's imagination or are used fictitiously and are not to be construed as real. Any resemblance to actual events, locales, organizations, or persons, living or dead, is entirely coincidental.

◆

HARPERTORCH
An Imprint of HarperCollins*Publishers*
10 East 53rd Street
New York, New York 10022-5299

First HarperTorch paperback printing: July 2005

HarperCollins®, HarperTorch™, and ◆ ™ are trademarks of HarperCollins Publishers Inc.

Printed in the United States of America

Visit HarperTorch on the World Wide Web at www.harpercollins.com

10 9 8 7 6 5 4 3 2 1

RUNNING
IRONS

Chapter 1

BAT GOOCH'S MISTAKE

THERE WERE MANY TYPES OF MARKS BY WHICH THE
ranchers of the old west established ownership of
their cattle, ranging from straightforward initial or
number brands to John Chisum's Long Rail, a line
burned along the animal's side from rump to
shoulder.

A box brand had a square outline around letters
or numbers; a connected brand meant that one of
the letters in it touched the other; barbed brands
carried a short projection from some part of them;
a bench brand stood on a horizontal bracket with
legs extending downward like a bench; a drag
brand carried lines sticking downward from its
bottom; should a brand have a small extension

from each side it was said to be "flying"; a letter suspended from or connected to a quarter circle bore the title "swinging"; a tumbling brand meant that its letters leaned over at an oblique angle; a walking brand bore twin small extensions like feet at its lower extremities; a rafter brand sheltered under an inverted V-shape; a forked brand carried a small V-shaped prong on one of its sides; a running brand meant that flowing lines trailed from it; a bradded brand had a large termini; a collection of wings without a central figure bore the title "whangdoodle." *Hacienderos* below the Rio Grande used such large and complicated brands that a man might read them by moonlight, but could make no sense of them. The Texas cowhands called such brands "maps of Mexico," "skillets of snakes," "greaser madhouses" and other less complimentary names.

A red-hot branding iron alone served the purpose of applying such a mark of ownership to a man's stock. This consisted of a three-foot-long iron rod with a handle at one end and a reversed facsimile of the outfit's chosen brand at the other. Such a branding iron, when heated correctly and applied to the animal's hide, left a plain, easily read sign by which all men knew who owned the critter bearing it.

While riding the range on their lawful occasions cowhands often toted along one of their outfit's branding irons so as to be able to catch, tie down and mark any unclaimed stock they came across. It might be a grown animal overlooked in earlier roundups, or a new-born, late-dropped calf running at its mother's side. Either way the application of the outfit's brand set the seal of ownership upon the animal and added more potential wealth to the cowhand's ranch. So a cowhand who carried his outfit's iron was regarded as being a good worker, industrious and a man to be most highly commended.

But when a rider carried a rod without a stamp-head upon it, man, that was some different. Known as a running iron, such a rod could be used to change the shape of a brand, or for "venting," running a line through the original mark so as to nullify it, then trace another brand upon the animal—done legally this was known as counter-branding and was used when a critter be wrongly branded or sold after receiving its owner's mark. So a man carrying a running iron was not thought of as being praiseworthy or commendable. Folks called him a cow thief.

For almost six months past the range country around Caspar County, Texas, had been plagued by cow thieves. Stock disappeared in numbers that were too great to be put down to inclement weather or the depredations of cougar, wolf or bear; besides, not even the great Texas grizzly ate the bones of its kills and no sign of animal kills led the ranchers to blame *Ursus Texensis Texensis* for their losses. No sir, a human agency lay behind the disappearances and the ranchers decided it to be long gone time that something was done. A man who worked damned hard, faced hunger, danger, gave his blood and sweat to raise himself above his fellows, and took the responsibility of ownership and development instead of being content to draw another's wages did not take kindly to having his property stolen from him. So the ranchers decided to strike back.

Of course there were ways and ways of striking back. Vic Crither's hiring of Bat Gooch struck most folks as going maybe a mite too far, even against cow thieves. Few bounty hunters ever achieved a higher social standing than Digger Indians and the Digger was reckoned as being the lowest of the low. Bat Gooch had a name for being worse than most of the men who hunted down fellow humans for the price their hide carried. For all that, Bat Gooch came to Caspar, called in by the mysterious, but highly effective prairie telegraph. Crither let it be known that Gooch would receive a flat wage for prowling the Forked C's range and a bonus of two hundred dollars each time he brought in a proven rustler—alive or dead.

The threat appeared to be working, for Gooch had ridden the ranges of the Forked C each night during the past fortnight without finding any sign of the cow thieves who preyed on the other ranches. While Vic Crither felt highly pleased with his strategy, the same could not be said for Gooch. So far his trip did not meet with his idea of the fitness of things. The potent quality of Gooch's name appeared to have scared the cow thieves from Forked C and not a single two hundred dollar bounty had so far come his way.

Being a man who liked money and all the good things it brought, Gooch decided, although he had never heard of the term, that if the mountain would not come to the prophet, then he would danged well go right out and find it for himself.

So it came about that on a clear, moonlit night Bat Gooch left the Forked C range and rode into the Bench J's domain. There was something about Gooch which warned of his chosen field of endeavor; a hint of cruelty and evil about his dark face and strangely pale eyes; the perpetual sneer on his lips, that silent way of moving, all hinted at something sinister. He wore dark clothing of cowhand style and Indian moccasins on his feet. In his saddleboot rode a Sharps Old Reliable buffalo rifle with a telescopic sight, but no bison had ever tumbled before its bullets. An Army Colt hung at his right side, a sheathed bowie knife on the left of his belt. Men had died through each of his weapons. In many ways Gooch was a man ideally suited to his work. He could move in silence through the thickest bush; shot well and possessed that rarest ability of being able to squeeze the trigger and kill another human being without a single hesitative thought. In addition to keen eyesight and excellent hearing, Gooch possessed a nose as sharp as a hound dog's.

On this occasion it was the nose which served him first. For four hours he had been prowling the Bench J land, eyes and ears alert for any sound that might guide him to a cow thief engaged in illegal operations. Once found, the cow thief would die and be taken on to the Forked C's range where his body commanded a price of two hundred dollars. Yet, though he searched with care and used a considerable knowledge of the working of cow thieves to direct him, Gooch found no sign during the first four hours.

Then it happened!

The wind carried a scent to him. Not the pleasant aroma of jasmine or roses, but one just as sweet to Gooch's keen nostrils. Raw, acrid and unmistakable it came, the stench of singed hair and burning cow hide as a branding iron seared its irremovable mark on to an animal. Yet no sound followed the stench. No sudden bleat of pain such as one heard when a brand was applied in normal circumstances. Not that folks branded cattle by night under normal circumstances—especially on a range troubled by cow thieves.

Two things were plain to Gooch: first, from the stench of burned hide somebody had just branded an animal upwind of him; second, the fact that the branders worked at night and took the trouble to muffle the branded critter's head and stop its bellow of pain told that they had good reason for not wishing to attract attention to themselves. Add one and two together, and the answer came out as a chance of picking up at least two hundred fine old U.S. dollars over and above Gooch's regular wages.

Keeping his big, wild-looking dark roan horse to an easy walk, its hooves hardly making a sound in the hock deep grass, Gooch rode up wind like a blue-tick hound going in on a breast-scent instead of running the line by the smell on the ground. Faint sounds came to his ears, then he saw a small glow of light flickering through the bushes and down a slope ahead of him. Once again his nostrils detected the smell of burning flesh and he brought his horse to a halt. Swinging from the saddle, he moved forward on foot. The big horse followed on his heels, stepping with all the silent caution of a whitetail deer in hard-hunted country. Give Gooch his due, he could train a horse and the roan ideally suited his purposes. Moving silently through the bushes, man and horse came into sight of a scene which did Gooch's money-hungry heart good to see.

At the foot of a small hollow six hundred dollars worth of cow thieves worked at their trade. The ground at the bottom of the small basin was clear of bushes, although its sides and the range around was liberally dotted with them and offered good cover which hid the light of the fire from all but the closest inspection. If Gooch had not caught the tell-tale smell of burning hide, he might have ridden right by the place without noticing anything. Instead he looked down at the three shapes around the fire. All wore cowhand clothes, although Gooch could only see two faces, the other having a wide-brimmed hat that effectively shielded the features. The two Gooch could see, he identified as young cowhands who worked for the Bench J; a brace of cheery, happy-go-lucky youngsters typical of hundreds across the length and breadth of the Texas range country. Although both of them wore holstered Colts, Gooch did not figure them as dangerous with the weapons—even if he aimed to give them a chance to fight. The third figure was smaller, not more than five seven, and slim under the wolf-skin jacket. Gooch studied all three noticing first that the slim, boyish third member of the party did not appear to be wearing a gunbelt.

Bending, the third figure thrust a running iron into the flames of the fire where a second iron lay heating. One of the other pair released a freshly branded calf and stripped the slicker from around its head.

"Go get another," said the third cow thief, nodding to where half-a-dozen calves stood hobbled.

Excitement appeared to be affecting that one, making his voice almost as high pitched as a soprano woman's. Gooch gave little thought to the voice, being more concerned with deciding what course of action to take and which of his armament best suited his purpose. The single-shot Sharps would not serve, nor the bowie, so he must handle things with his Colt. At that range, with his targets illuminated by a fire, he figured to be able to down all three. If he knew them, they would panic when the first one went down, giving him a chance to tumble the other two before they could make for the trio of horses standing at the far side of the clearing. He reached down a big right hand, drawing the 1860 Army Colt from its holster.

"I don't like this," the taller of the trio stated, standing with his back to Gooch—although he did not know of the bounty hunter's presence.

"Nor me," the second cowhand went on. "Buck Jerome's been a good boss."

"Shucks, he'll not miss a few head, and anyways you know you can slap a brand on any unbranded critter you see," the third member of the party answered.

"Sure," agreed the second rider. "Only this bunch were with Bench J cows."

"So?" snorted the third cow thief. "That doesn't mean they had Bench J mammies. And anyways, how'll you and Dora ever save en——"

The words ended unsaid as flame spurted from the darkness of the bush-dotted slopes around the basin. Caught in the middle of the back by a .44 caliber soft lead round ball—so much more deadly in impact and effect than a conical bullet—the tallest member of the trio pitched forward and just missed the fire as he fell. Just as Gooch figured, the second cowhand showed shocked indecision for an instant before trying to turn and draw his gun. By that time Gooch had cocked the Colt on its recoil and, before the young cowhand completed his turn or made his fumbling draw, fired again. Lead ripped into the cowhand's head, dropping him in a lifeless heap on the ground, his gun still in leather.

At which point Gooch saw that his plan had partially gone wrong. Instead of being in a state of panic, the third member of the party acted with speed and a show of planned thought. Spinning around, the figure left the fire and sped toward the horses in a fast, swerving run. Twice Gooch's Colt roared, but his bullets missed their mark. With a bound, the escaping cow thief went afork one of the horses. Range trained, the horse had been standing untied, its reins dangling before it. Scooping up the reins, the cow thief set the horse running, crashed it through the surrounding bushes like they were not there.

Still holding his Colt, Gooch turned and vaulted into his saddle. Knowing its work, the roan leapt forward, racing down the slope and across the open ground. A glance in passing told Gooch that he had earned four hundred dollars and that if not already dead the two cowhands soon would be. Knowing he could safely leave them where they lay, and find them there on his return, Gooch gave his full attention to riding down the last member of the trio.

Through the bushes and out on to the open range tore the horses, one ridden by a cow thief with the fear of death, the other carrying the same death in human form, wearing range clothes instead of a night-shirt and toting a .44 Army Colt in place of the more conventional scythe. For almost half a mile Gooch chased the cow thief, his roan closing the gap with every raking stride, although the other's mount was not exactly slow. While the bounty hunter held his Colt, he did not attempt to shoot. Gooch knew the folly of trying to shoot from the back of a running horse, at least over anything but short range. Sure, he had two loaded chambers left, but recharging a percussion-fired revolver could not be done from the back of a racing horse, and he had no wish to approach the other when holding an empty gun. So he aimed to get closer in and cut loose from a range where he could not miss; or if the worst came to the worst, take the fleeing rider from the ground and using his heavy caliber rifle.

Once the fleeing cow thief twisted in the saddle and looked back, gauging the distance between them and guessing there was no chance of outrunning that big roan. Turning to the front again, the rider reached up with a hand to open the jacket and do something else that Gooch could not see. The bounty hunter grunted, not unduly worried, for he knew shooting backward from a galloping horse to be, if anything, even less accurate than firing in a forward direction. However, a man did not care to take chances on catching a stray bullet; he could be killed just as long, permanently, dead by a blind-lucky shot as through one taken after careful and deliberate aim.

Before the bounty hunter could make his move, either to start using the Colt or stop the roan, dismount and make use of his Sharps, he saw what appeared to be a stroke of bad luck take the fleeing rider. Ahead of the cow thief stood a noble old cottonwood; the spreading branches of which no stealer of cattle ought to look on without a shudder and thinking of the hairy touch of a Manila rope around the neck. However, the rider appeared to be mighty insensitive to atmosphere, for the horse's course took it under the low, wide spread branches of the tree.

Suddenly the cow thief jerked backward, apparently struck by a branch, and slid over the horse's rump to crash to the ground. Gooch brought his roan to a halt, gun held ready for use as he studied the shape on the ground. Swinging from his saddle, Gooch advanced and the shape moved slowly, rolling on to its back. Gooch's Colt had lined at the first movement, its hammer drawn back ready and his forefinger on the trigger. Before he could send lead crashing into the near-helpless shape, he saw something that made him hold his fire and brought a broader sneer than usual to his lips.

In falling, the cow thief's hat had gone from his head and the shirt under the thrown-open jacket appeared to have been torn apart to expose the flesh below. The first thing Gooch noticed was long hair trailing around the head. Hair far longer than even Wild Bill Hickok sported, and framing a beautiful, most unmasculine face. Next the bounty hunter's eyes strayed downward, to the open shirt and what it exposed. Apparently the cow thief did not go in for wearing underclothing and what Gooch could see rising from the open shirt most certainly did not belong to any man.

Holstering his gun, Gooch walked forward and drank in the sight of those round, full and naked female breasts. Never a pleasant sight, his evil face looked even more so as he advanced on the moaning, agony-moving figure. While watching the trio by the fire Gooch had been aware that this third member of the party appeared to be the boss. Maybe she was the boss rustler of the area. Stranger things had happened and from what Gooch had seen of her in Caspar, she had the brains to be the big augur and nobody would ever suspect her. Only now she had been caught in the act and would bring in at least two hundred dollars same as the other two—dead.

Only before she died, Gooch figured he might as well pleasure himself a mite. He had a keen eye for a beautiful face and good figure; and, man, that gal on the ground afore him possessed both. Once dead, which she would be as soon as he finished his fun, the girl could not tell any tales of what happened before she met her end.

"Gal," he said, dropping to his knees besides her and reaching down toward the open shirt front, "if you enjoy it, you'll sure die hap——"

Which same concluded his speech, although he had not entirely finished it. Suddenly the girl jerked her right hand into sight, it having been hidden under her jacket, a Remington Double Derringer gripped firmly in her fingers. Taken completely by surprise, Gooch looked death in the face. Shocked horror crossed his features and wiped the leering lust from them. Even as he tried to force his brain into positive, cohesive thought, to lurch erect, grab out his Colt, try to knock aside the wicked, deadly .41 caliber hideout gun, do anything at all to save his life, the sands of time ran out for Bat Gooch.

The Derringer spat once, its bullet taking Gooch just under the breast bone and ranging upward. While the Double Derringer's three-inch barrels, comparatively weak powder charge and large caliber bullet did not have great carrying or penetrative powers over a range of thirty yards, Gooch was well within its killing area. A tearing, numbing agony ripped through Gooch, stopping his hand even before it could claw out his gun. Again the Derringer roared, its second bullet slicing into Gooch's body. Rearing to his feet, Gooch stood for a moment and then tumbled over backward.

Coming to her feet, the woman reloaded the Double Derringer and dropped it into her jacket pocket. Without a glance at the dying man, she buttoned her shirt and closed the jacket over it.

"I figured you'd fall for that, you lousy murdering skunk," she remarked, picking up and putting on her hat.

Her horse had come to a halt a short distance away and she walked to it. Taking the reins, she set a foot into the stirrup iron and swung gracefully into her saddle. Ignoring Gooch as if he did not exist—and he no longer did except as a lump of lifeless flesh—the woman rode back in the direction from which she fled.

Back at the hollow, the woman showed no more interest in the two dead cowhands than she had for Gooch's welfare. Swinging from the saddle, she stood for a moment and thought out the situation. First those half-a-dozen calves must be released. It was a pity they had only branded three of the animals. Alone she could not handle the branding of the others. Besides somebody might have heard the shooting and even now be riding to investigate. Shots in the dark on the Caspar County range would attract more attention under the prevailing conditions than normally and she had no wish to be caught. Being a smart woman, she did not regard the ranchers as fools, or figure they could not think things out. Maybe they might not be able to prove anything against her, but they sure would be suspicious to see *her* of all people riding the range at night and dressed in man's clothing. She would be watched too carefully in future to carry on with this profitable side-line to her normal business and that was the last thing she wanted.

Taking up a knife one of the cowhands had tossed into the dirt so as to be handy for hurried freeing of the calves, the woman walked forward and released the unbranded animals. As she expected, they wasted no time in heading off through the bushes, blatting loudly and looking for their mothers. She collected the two dead cowhands' ropes and with her own secured the three branded calves to her saddlehorn. After cutting the calves' hobbles, she mounted the horse.

"Hard luck, boys," she said, throwing a glance at the two shapes by the dying fire. "That's life for you."

And with no more sentiment than that, the woman rode away, leading the three calves behind her. She left behind two dead cowhands—and two running irons.

Chapter 2

SHE'S A MIGHTY SMART WOMAN

~⌒~⌒~

STANTON HOWARD, GOVERNOR OF THE STATE OF Texas, was a busy man who could quite well have done without the cow thief problem of Caspar County being dumped in his lap. Brought in after the Texans' forcible ejection of Carpetbag Davis' corrupt, vicious Reconstruction administration, Howard found enough work to last him a solid twenty-four hours a day—he could have worked twenty-six hours a day if that be possible and still find work to do in plenty the following morning.

The disbanding of Davis' State Police had brought problems in its wake. For several years there had been little State law enforcement in Texas, Davis' men being more concerned with lining their own pockets in the guise of elevating the Negro to the status of a citizen with equal rights. With the departure of the State Police commanders—or such of them who did not meet not undeserved fates on the end of a rope—the colored policemen slipped back to their homes, or wandered northward in search of a land flowing with milk and honey. In the place of the State Police, the Texas Rangers returned from their Davis-inspired removal. Honest men, many of whom could have earned far more than their Ranger's wages in other, less dangerous walks of life, joined. The Texas Rangers asked little of its recruits other than loyalty, courage, ability to ride anything with four legs and hair and the knowledge of how to handle firearms.

However, with every Ranger working full time, Howard could well have done without receiving the letter from Caspar County. Yet one of the Governor's most pressing duties was to appease those Texans—and there were many—who had developed a hearty hatred of authority as represented by Washington's appointed head of the State. Knowing Texans, for he belonged to the Lone Star State himself, Howard could read between the lines of the letter. He smelled trouble in the air, far more trouble than one might expect from the theft of a few cows.

A jerk on the bell cord hanging behind him

brought one of Howard's hard-working secretaries into the well-furnished room.

"Get Captain Murat for me," the Governor said.

Five minutes later the door opened and a tall, slim, dark man in his early thirties entered. Although Captain Jules Murat, commander of Troop "G," Texas Rangers, wore town clothes, he carried himself with the swing of a horseman. One might almost imagine him wearing a plumed, cocked hat, a cloak over a Hussar uniform, a saber at his side instead of a brace of holstered 1860 Army Colts, for there was a Gasconading air about him, a hint of controlled, deadly recklessness. Tanned, handsome, very rich, Murat was still one of the best Ranger captains under Howard's command.

"Trouble, Jules," Howard said, waving Murat into a chair and offering his cigar case.

"No thanks," replied Murat, taking a cigar. "We've plenty of our own."

"I hate a humorist at this hour of the day," grunted the Governor.

"And me. What kind of trouble have you for me this time, Stan?"

"Cow thieves."

Clipping the end off his cigar, Murat looked down at the weed. Although he showed nothing of his emotions, Murat had been sweating out the thought that the trouble might be yet another blood feud sprung out of the hatreds left behind by Davis' administration. Man, there you had real Texas-size trouble. With an entire county taking one side or the other, it was surely hell trying to discover the rights and wrongs of the affair, locate and arrest killers from either faction and pacify the rest before more blood spilled.

"There's plenty of them around," he remarked, showing remarkable tolerance for a man who owned a good-sized spread and large herd.

"Small stuff," stated the Governor. "It's gone beyond being small up to Caspar County, Jules."

Watching Howard, the Ranger captain felt his usual admiration. Sigmund Freud had not yet got around to presenting his views on human mentality to the world so, not knowing he should subconsciously hate his employer, Murat was willing to respect Howard as a brilliant man doing a difficult task. No matter what happened in Texas, sooner or later—and mostly sooner—Howard heard of it. More than that, the Governor formed his own conclusions from what he heard and mostly those conclusions proved to be correct. Mostly Howard left the Rangers to their own devices. When he called in one of the captains commanding the various companies, it meant Howard felt more than usually concerned about some incident or other.

"I smell bad trouble brewing up there, Jules,"

the Governor went on. "Vic Crither's passed word for Bat Gooch."

"That *is* asking for trouble," Murat admitted, almost showing the concern he felt. "What's Gooch been fetched in to do?"

"Get the cow thieves—at two hundred dollars a head."

Murat did not hold down his low whistle. "That trouble you smell, I can get scent of it now. Gooch'll not be content just to ride Crither's range and let his name scare off any festive jasper with a running iron. He'll go out looking for the cow thieves no matter whose land they're working on."

"You're right," Howard agreed. "With a man like Gooch riding the range, trouble's just over the rim and in peeking out ready to come boiling over. Bringing Gooch in's like turning loose a rabid dog to hunt down coyotes."

"No man likes to see his property stole from under him," Murat remarked.

"Which same I'll give you," Howard replied. "But there are better ways of stopping it than fetching in professional killers. Like you say, Gooch's not going to be content with just scaring the cow thieves off, he's there after a bounty. Only if he goes on to some other range, or downs an innocent man, he'll blow up all hell. I want action on this, Jules—and I want it fast."

When Murat nodded his agreement he was not merely giving lip-service. After nine months in office together, Murat had learned to respect Howard's judgment and knew the Governor's insistence on immediate action did not spring from either panic or vote catching. Howard knew Texans, knew their high temper, their loyalty to kin or ranch. Already two bloody feuds and range wars ripped at Texas counties and none knew the cost in lives and misery they brought to the suffering citizens of the areas involved. Another such affair could start those fools in Washington thinking about trying to reinstitute Reconstruction and, by cracky, that might be enough to restart the Civil War. Texas, least affected Southern State in the war, a nation of born fighting men who learned to handle weapons almost before they could walk, had never taken kindly to Reconstruction or having the "if he's black he's right" policies of the Radical-Republicans up North forced on them. Another non-Texan governor, such as Davis might see the entire State torn apart by further civil conflict. Other than the most bigoted, Southern-hating, liberal-intellectual Yankees, no man in his right mind wanted that.

"It needs action," the Ranger captain drawled.

"But?" asked Howard. "There's a 'but' in your voice."

"I've only three men in camp out of my entire company. One with a broken arm, one with a bullet-busted thigh and the third's flat on his back with lead in his chest cavity."

"Three—out of twenty?"

"The rest are all out handling chores," Murat explained and went on hopefully, "Shall I go?"

"I can't spare you, Jules. You're needed here, organizing and attending to enlisting more recruits."

"Danged if I don't resign and re-enlist as a private. I'll send off the first of my men to come in. Although the Lord knows when that'll be."

"Let's hope it will be soon," the Governor answered.

Clearly the interview had ended and Howard never wasted time in idle chatter. Coming to his feet, Murat turned and walked from the office. Before the Ranger reached the door, Howard had taken up a report from an Army commander and started to study the problem of controlling the Comanche Indians.

On leaving the Governor's office, Murat collected his horse and rode down town toward the Ranger barracks which housed Company "G." Once clear of the State Capital's area, Austin looked pretty much like any other cattle town. Rising along the wheel-rutted, dirt-surfaced street, Murat gave thought to his problem. No matter how much he wished to take action and, if possible, prevent another range war blowing up, he could do nothing until one of his men returned from the various tasks which held their attention.

A small, two-horse wagon came slowly along the street toward Murat. In passing, its driver—a tall, thin, dirty-looking bearded man in a frock coat, top hat, dirty collarless white shirt and old pants—caught Murat's eye and gave a slight jerk of his head. So slight had been the motion that a less observant man than Murat would have missed it. Even seeing the nod, Murat gave no sign but rode slowly on. After passing Murat, the man turned his wagon and drove it along an alley between two buildings. Murat rode on a short way before swinging his horse into the space between a saloon and its neighboring barber's shop. Beyond the buildings lay a small, deserted street and the wagon had halted along it. Riding up to the halted wagon, Murat looked down to where its driver stood examining a wheel.

"In trouble, Jake?" he asked.

"Danged wheel's near on coming off," the man replied.

"Let me take a look."

Swinging from his horse, Murat walked to the wagon and bent down to inspect its wheel. Doing so put his face near to the man and the stench of unwashed flesh wafted to his nostrils. Murat wondered if Jacob Jacobs ever took soap and water to his hide, but did not ask. Jacobs was a pedlar, but who augmented his takings by acting as a gatherer and seller of information garnered in his travels around the range.

"You interested in running irons, Cap'n?" Jacobs asked in a low voice, bringing up the matter in the middle of a louder tirade about the poor quality of workmanship in the fitting of the wheel.

"Depends where they are," Murat answered.

"Up to Caspar County."

"I'm interested. What do you know?"

"I'm a poor man, Cap'n. There's no money to be made by a poor old Jewish pedlar these days."

"Or a Ranger captain," Murat countered.

"Heard about all the trouble and went up there special, me being a public-spirited citizen and all," Jacobs put in. "It's allus been poor trading country up there and I lost business."

"Who's behind the stealing?" Murat asked, cutting off any further descriptions of Jacobs's self-sacrifice.

"A woman."

It said much for Murat's self-control that he showed no emotion at the words even though disbelief welled in him. His eyes studied Jacobs's face, but he read nothing in the pedlar's expression.

"Does she have a name?" Murat asked.

"Like I said, Cap'n, I'm a poor man."

Taking out his wallet, Murat peeled off a ten-dollar bill and slipped it into a grimy palm that engulfed it like a large-mouth bass sucking in a shiner minnow.

"Who is it?"

"Name of Ella Watson. She runs the Cattle Queen."

"Can you prove it?" asked Murat.

"Proof the man wants!" yelped Jacobs in what, if possible, was a *sotto voce* wail of protest. "I tell him who is—I tell you, Cap'n, you Rangers should ought to arrest the feller who sold me this wagon."

The last words came out in a much louder, complaining tone as a man walked from an alley behind them and passed by. Like all informers, Jacobs knew full well the delicate nature of his position and the danger it involved. He had no wish to become known as one who passed on confidential information to law enforcement officers and took all precautions possible to avoid raising suspicions. Not until the man had passed out of hearing distance did either the pedlar or the Ranger captain resume their conversation.

"I sure as hell haven't had ten bucks worth yet," Murat warned as the other seemed inclined to edge around the question of proof.

Which same proved to be a powerful argument and one which Jacobs could understand right well. He knew Murat paid high for information, but expected service and accuracy in return for the money spent.

"I don't know much about it," Jacobs admitted. "Wasn't there for more than two days, pulled out as soon as I learned who was behind it. I figgered you'd want to know as soon as I could make it."

"Likely. Who-all's in it with her?"

"She gets some of the fool young cowhands to do the stealing. The young 'uns who haven't got too much good sense but like to feel a gal's leg now and then. Pays them for what they steal and gets the money back in her place when she's paid them. She's a might smart woman, Cap'n."

"Sounds that way," Murat grunted. "Nothing more you can tell me?"

"Not about her. Don't know where she gets shut of the stuff once it's been stolen or even where she keeps it while she's waiting to sell."

That figured to anybody who knew Jacobs. While the man willingly sold his information, he never took any extra chances in gathering it. However, Murat decided he had a start, a point where whichever man he sent up to Caspar County could make a beginning in breaking the spate of cow stealing. There was another point, a matter of some importance which Jacobs failed to mention.

"How about Bat Gooch?"

"He's been there for just over a week and—how'd you know about him?"

"My mother had a voodoo-mama nurse," Murat answered, cursing the slowness of the mails. When Governor Howard's letter was dispatched Gooch still had not arrived in Caspar. Not that Murat intended to enlighten Jacobs; it did the Ranger captain's prestige no harm to have Jacobs think he knew more than his actual knowledge. "Has he done anything?"

"Not much. Hasn't made him a bounty yet that anybody knows about. Crither's saying his losses've been cut already though."

Strange as it may seem, the news did not relieve Murat's anxiety as much as one might expect it to. If the fear inspired by Gooch's name and evil reputation had scared the cow thieves off the Forked C range, the bounty hunter ought to be spreading the sphere of his activities real soon. From what he knew of Gooch, Murat reckoned the man would not be content with just wages and was likely to seek out victims on the neighboring ranges. Sure, Murat wanted to drive the cow thieves off the range and stop their activities, which Gooch's presence might do—but there was such a thing as the price being too high. The sooner the Ranger captain could send one of his men to Caspar, the better he would feel. Even one Ranger on the ground might act as a steadying influence and prevent Gooch from going too far in his bounty-hunting search for wealth.

"There's a couple more gunhands hanging around town," Jacobs remarked. "Are on Ella Watson's pay-roll, I think. They don't say much, or do much. 'Course, they only came in the day afore I left."

Once again the pedlar gave Murat worrying news. Hired guns always meant bad trouble. If Ella Watson had brought in a couple of guns, it might be for the purpose of nullifying the threat Gooch offered to her cow-stealing business—always assuming that Jacobs had his facts right and she did run the she-bang.

Without letting his concern show, Murat slipped another five dollars into Jacobs's hand. "If you go south, see if you can learn anything about those stage robberies they've had down that way," he said.

"Sure, Cap'n. How about that Caspar fuss?"

"I'll send word to the sheriff up there and let him do what he wants."

"Aren't you sending your men in?" Jacobs inquired.

"Only if the local law asks for them," replied Murat cagily.

While Jacobs had proved himself a reliable source of information on more than one occasion, Murat did not trust the man. Knowledge of the coming of a Ranger, or a party of Rangers, would fetch a good price from the right area and Jacobs might just as easily sell his news to the cow thieves as he had to Murat. So Murat did not intend to give too much away; not with the lives of his men at stake.

"Don't reckon he'll ask," grinned Jacobs. "Sheriff Simmonds ain't the best, or smartest, lawman in the West."

"He getting paid for sitting back and doing nothing?"

"I couldn't say, Cap'n. Only he's sure dressing better now than he did last time I saw him, before the cow stealing started."

"I likely won't hear anything from him then," Murat grunted. "Which same I've paid out fifteen iron men for nothing."

"News is always valuable, Cap'n," answered Jacobs.

"So they do tell me," agreed the Ranger. "See you, Jake."

"I'll be around," promised the pedlar. "You wanting me to go down south and see what I can find about the stage hold-ups?"

"If you're headed that way—and afore you ask, don't. You've made fifteen bucks off me for something I might not be able to put to use."

Turning, Murat walked to his horse and swung into the saddle. Jacobs watched the Ranger captain ride away and then swung aboard his wagon. With an annoyed sniff, the pedlar started his team moving. He felt disappointment at not learning more about Murat's plans. The Ranger captain most likely aimed to send at least one of his men to Caspar and to be able to identify the man might have proved profitable. Ella Watson would have paid well to know of her danger and be able to recognize it when the Ranger arrived. One thing Jacobs learned early was never to try to sell half information to criminals. While Ella Watson might be interested to know that the Rangers were coming, she was unlikely to pay for the information—at least not enough to make a return trip to Caspar worthwhile—unless Jacobs could also tell who exactly to watch for.

Murat rode between the two buildings and back on to the street once more, turning over the problem and Jacobs's information in his mind. A worried frown creased his face as he continued his interrupted return to his company's barracks. One thing was even more sure now. The Governor had been right to worry about the developments in Caspar County. Cow stealing was bad enough; but when both sides started importing hired killers the situation became far worse.

Hoping against hope, Murat swung his horse through the gates into the compound of Troop "G," Texas Rangers. No imposingly military structure lay before him. The compound had no parade ground, for the Rangers did no drill and wore no uniform. Just an adobe office building and cells, three wooden cabins, a long stable and barn, and a pole corral made up the company's headquarters. Murat glanced hopefully at the corral, but found it to be empty. The company's remuda had been taken out on to the range beyond the compound to graze and any horse in the corral would mean that one of his men was back from a chore.

Even as a youngster, one of the trio who acted as wranglers for the Rangers' horses, dashed up to collect Murat's mount, a tall man in cowhand clothes and with his right arm suspended in a sling left the office building. The man walked toward Murat and the captain asked:

"No sign of any of the boys, Sid?"

"Nope. I'm near on fit though."

The injured Ranger knew a summons from the Governor meant something urgent and wondered what further trouble had been heaped on Murat's shoulders.

"Near on's not good enough, Sid. I can't send you out until you can handle a rifle as well as a Colt."

"Danged spoilsport," growled Sid, but he knew Murat to be right. A Ranger with a bullet-busted wing sure would be at a disadvantage in handling any risky law work. "It bad?"

"Bad enough," admitted Murat. "Let's go in and I'll tell you about it."

Following Sid into the office, Murat made a decision. Unless at least one of his men had returned by sundown the following day, Murat intended to disregard the Governor's orders and head for Caspar himself.

Chapter 3

MISS CANARY IN DISTRESS

~~~

Miss Martha Jane Canary expected to be raped and killed before fifteen more minutes went by. Already the sweat-stinking fat cuss had finished his food and started opening the drawers of the side-piece, grinning slyly at her and waiting for her objections. The handsome jasper, if you cared for swarthy features and a drooping moustache, the others called Choya still sat eating; his black eyes studying the girl as if trying to strip her with his gaze. After finishing his meal, the short, scar-faced *hombre* named Gomez had left the cabin on a visit to the backhouse and the fourth member of that evil quartet, Manuel, sat wolfing down a mess of victuals like it was going out of style. When they all had finished eating and no longer required her services as cook, the ball was sure as hell going to start.

From the first moment she saw the four Mexicans riding toward the cabin, the girl expected trouble. One saw plenty of Mexicans in this part of Texas, but the quartet struck her as being wrong. While they dressed to the height of *vaquero* fashion, they showed a mean-faced, slit-eyed wolf caution which did not go with the behavior of such Mexican cowhands she had seen on her travels. The backward glances, the careful, alert scrutiny of the place as they rode toward it, each told the girl a story. She knew instinctively the four men riding toward her were bad. Outlaws of some sort; maybe *Comancheros,* those human wolves who preyed on both white and Indian, leaving a trail of carnage wherever they went. All but smashed by the Texas Rangers before the Civil War, a few small bands of *Comancheros* had avoided capture, or sprung into being during Davis' incompetent administration. It seemed in keeping with the girl's general lousy luck of the past few days that she should run across one such bunch under the present conditions.

Way she looked at it, only one good thing could be said of the situation. Those four snake-eyed greasers did not know her true identity. They must take her for the wife or, as she wore no rings, daughter of the house; easy meat for their evil purposes once she had filled their bellies. Most likely they would not have been so relaxed, or taken such chances, had they known her to be Calamity Jane.

Not that Calamity looked quite her usual self. She had seen to that on taking stock of her position in respect of the approaching riders. Her hat, a faded old U.S. cavalry kepi, hung behind the door instead of perching at its usual jaunty angle on her mop of curly red hair. Nothing about her tanned, slightly freckled, pretty face gave a hint of her true identity; the eyes were merry most time, the lips looked made for laughing and kissing, but could turn loose a blistering flow of team-driver's invective at times. The man's shirt she wore looked maybe two sizes too small as it clung to her rich, round, full bosom and slender waist, its neck open maybe just a mite lower than some folks regarded as seemly, the sleeves rolled up to show strong-looking arms. However, she wore a black skirt from the waist down, effectively covering her levis pants; the latter, like the shirt, fitted a mite snug and drew sniffs of disapproval from good ladies when Calamity passed by. Not that Calamity usually gave a damn about how folks regarded her style of dress. She wore men's clothing because she did a man's job and only donned the skirt as a piece of simple disguise which appeared to have fooled the four Mexicans.

Calamity had been on her way to Austin with a wagon-load of supplies, handling a contract for her boss, Dobe Killem, and decided to call in to visit with her friends, Dai and Blodwin Jones. On her arrival she found the Jones' had gone into Austin that morning, but with frontier hospitality they left the house open and food around for any chance-passing stranger to take a meal. Being hungry and trail-dirty, Calamity decided to night at the house. After caring for the team which drew her big Conestoga wagon, Calamity took a bath in the Jones family's swimming hole behind the house— leaving her gunbelt with its ivory butted Navy Colt, Winchester carbine and bull whip in the boot of the wagon. Like a danged fool green kid fresh out from the East, she did not collect the weapons before entering the house and cooking up a meal.

Not until she heard the hooves of the Mexicans' horses and looked from the window did Calamity realize the full gravity of her mistake. One glance told the range-wise Calamity all she needed to know about the visitors and she did not like the thought. The Jones' had taken their weapons with them when they headed for town. Nobody left guns, ammunition, powder and lead around an empty house. Even so close to Austin, capital city of the State of Texas, there was always a chance of an Indian raid and no Texan wanted to present a bunch of hostiles with free firearms. Calamity did not even consider using one of the butcher knives to defend herself. Mexicans were a nation of knife-fighters and she would have no chance against them using cold steel. Nor did she commit the folly of dashing out to her wagon. Before she could make it, the *Comancheros* would be on her.

Thinking fast, Calamity headed for the Jones' bedroom and grabbed one of Blodwin's skirts. Blodwin stood a few inches taller than Calamity and the extra length of the skirt hid the fact that Calamity wore men's pants and Pawnee moccasins, then she waited for the Mexicans to arrive.

On their arrival, the four men had been all politeness. Choya, he appeared to be their leader, greeted her in fair English, asking if the *señorita* could feed four poor travellers. All the time he spoke, his three men scanned the place with careful eyes, searching for sign of the male members of the household and sitting with their hands on gun butts. On receiving Calamity's permission to enter, the Mexicans left their horses standing outside, not fastened but with trailing reins to prevent the animals straying. Calamity cooked up a meal of ham and eggs, conscious of the evil, lust-filled eyes watching her every move. There had been a knowing, mocking sneer on Choya's lips as he listened to her remarks about the ranch's crew being due back at any moment; he knew her to be alone and, as he thought, real helpless.

Carefully avoiding turning to where the fat man searched the side-piece's drawers, Calamity watched and waited. With the meal all but over, she figured it would not be long before the men decided to make their play. If she hoped to come out of the affair with her life, she must act soon, fast and right.

"There's nothing here, Choya," the fat man stated in Spanish. "No money, no guns. Nothing for us."

"She may know where there is something," Choya answered. "It will be amusing to find out, hey, Manuel?"

Swallowing a mouthful of food, the fourth member of the party ogled Calamity with evil eyes. "It will," he agreed. "Who is first?"

"Me," said the fat man.

"You was first last time, Ramon," Manuel objected.

Calamity knew it was now or never. While the conversation had been in Spanish, which she did not speak, her instincts warned her of its meaning. One did not need the powers of a Pawnee witch-woman to figure out what lay in the Mexicans' minds, it showed too plainly on their faces for that.

Slowly she lifted the lid of the coffeepot, as if to check on the level of its contents. Among other unladylike things, her freight outfit friends had taught her a thorough working knowledge of the game of poker, including the art of hiding the emotions; and she used all her skill to prevent herself giving any hint of her intentions. Ramon still stood at the far side of the room by the side-piece and, if Calamity be any kind of judge on such matters, his holster did not look to be the type from which a Colt could be drawn speedily. Of the two men at the table, Choya struck Calamity as being the most dangerous and the one to be taken out of the game first.

With that thought in mind, Calamity acted. Suddenly, and without giving a hint of her intentions, she hurled the contents of the coffeepot into Choya's face. Almost half a pot full of very hot coffee caught the man, temporarily blinding him. Jerking back, hands clawing at his face, Choya threw over his chair and crashed to the floor.

Manuel gave an explosive Spanish curse, shoving his chair back and starting to rise. Even as the man's hand went toward his gun, Calamity, moving with the speed of urgent desperation, turned from Choya and met the fresh menace. Pivoting around, Calamity swung her arm at and crashed the bottom of the coffeepot into Manuel's face. Calamity had worked hard ever since her sixteenth birthday and had real strong arms. So as she hit to hurt, Manuel knew the blow landed. Blood gushing from his nose, Manuel went over backward smashing the chair under him and sprawled on to the floor.

With the two men at the table handled, Calamity gave Ramon her full and undivided attention. The fat man had been taken completely by surprise by the unexpected turn of events and, as Calamity figured, could not get out his gun with any speed. Not that he bothered; instead his hand dropped and drew a wicked, spear-pointed knife from its boot-top sheath. Whipping back her arm, Calamity hurled the coffeepot at Ramon's head and for a girl she could aim mighty straight. Even at the width of the cabin, the flying coffeepot landed hard enough to hurt and slowed down Ramon's attempt at retaliatory measures. The coffeepot's blow did little actual damage, but it brought Calamity a vital couple of seconds time—and at that moment every second gained was precious.

Snarling with rage, Ramon sprang forward. Not at the girl, but toward the door of the cabin; meaning to block her way out for Calamity was heading toward it. Only Calamity had already thought of and discarded the idea of using the door as a means of egress. Instead she headed for the window nearest to her. Covering her head with her arms, she hurled herself forward, passing through the window and taking both glass and sash with her. The way Calamity saw things, the Jones' window could be far more easily replaced than the damage those four yahoos would inflict should they lay hands on her.

Sailing through the window, Calamity lit down rolling like she had come off a bad horse. She went under the porch rail and landed on her feet beyond it. Wasting no time, she headed on the run for her wagon. From the corner of her eye, she saw the cabin door fly open and Ramon appeared. The Mexican came knife in hand, a trickle of blood running from his forehead where the coffeepot struck him.

Calamity reached the wagon and despite the awkwardness of wearing a skirt, leapt for the box. Even as she swung on to it, a glance to the rear told her how little time she had to save herself. Ramon had halted and already changed his hold on the knife, gripping it by the point of the blade instead of the hilt. While not the brightest of men, he could figure out that the girl did not head for the wagon in a state of blind panic. She must be after a weapon of some kind and he aimed to throw the knife, downing her before she reached whatever she sought in the wagon.

Grabbing for the nearest of her weapons, Calamity caught up the long bull whip's handle. Even as Ramon prepared to throw his knife, Calamity struck out. Her right hand rose, carrying the whip up and flicking its lash behind her. Down swept the arm, sending the whip's lash curling forward. An instant before Ramon made his throw, the tip of the lash caught him in the face, splattering his right eyeball as if it had been struck by the full force of a .44 bullet. Ramon screamed, the knife falling from his fingers as they clawed at his injured face.

For a moment Calamity thought that her luck had changed for the better. While she could handle her bull whip real well, there had not been time to take a careful aim. She just let fly and hoped for the best. Having a bull whip give its explosive pop within inches of one's head did not make for steady nerves or accurate aim when tossing a knife; so Calamity merely hoped to put Ramon off his aim, causing him to miss his throw, and give her the short time needed to change whip for carbine. From the way that fat jasper screeched and blood spurted between his fingers, she had done a whole lot better than just put him off by a near miss.

A bullet ripped the air by Calamity's head even as she swung around to drop the whip and grab up her Winchester. Once again, as she had several times before, Calamity decided there was no sound in the world she hated as much as the flat "splat!" sound of a close-passing bullet. Throwing a glance at the shooter, Calamity found she was not yet out of the woods. Gomez stood at the corner of the cabin, holding up his pants with one hand, lining his gun at her with the other. He stood well beyond the range of her whip and handled that smoking Starr Army revolver like he knew which end the bullets came from. What was more, he took careful aim, not meaning to miss again.

Letting the whip fall, Calamity prepared to make a grab that would see the twelve-shot Winchester Model '66 carbine in her hands—unless she took a .44 Starr bullet between the shoulders first. It had been her original intention to make the wagon, collect the carbine and fort up some place where she could have a clear field of fire at the front of the cabin. If the plan had succeeded, Calamity reckoned she ought to be able to hand those jaspers their needings.

Only she had forgotten Gomez and it seemed that her lack of foresight would cost her dearly. She doubted if he aimed to miss a second time. Nor would there be time for her to grab the carbine and stop him.

Even as death stared Calamity in the face, while the Mexican aimed his revolver and pressed its double-action trigger, a shot rang out. Not the deep boom of a handgun, but the crack of a Winchester rifle. For an instant Calamity thought her unseen rescuer had struck a flour-sack, for something white sprayed up from Gomez' head. Then she realized that the Winchester's bullet, on striking the skull, had shattered the bone, spraying slivers of it and pulped out brains flying into the air. The Starr fell from Gomez' hand as his body collapsed in a limp, boned-out manner to the ground.

Not that Calamity wasted any time in thinking about the sight. Already Choya and Manuel were coming through the cabin door and they looked mean as all hell. Each man held a gun and had murder in his heart, with Calamity as the one they aimed to kill.

Bending down, Calamity jerked the carbine from its boot fitted to the inside of the wagon box. The move saved her life for both Mexicans fired at her and the lead passed over her head. The roars of the revolvers mingled with yet another shot from her unseen rescuer's rifle. Swivelling around, carbine in hand, Calamity saw the effect of the second rifle bullet. Choya leaned against the door jamb, sliding slowly down. A trickle of blood ran from his chest and his Remington had fallen out of his hand.

Manuel saw Calamity swing toward him, the carbine held with practiced ease in her hands. For a moment he hesitated, wavering between handling the girl and locating the as yet unseen rifle-user. That indecision cost him his life, it gave the girl a vitally needed second or so in which to throw up and sight the rifle. Even as Manuel started to bring his revolver in her direction, Calamity shot him dead. She knew the *Comanchero* breed, knew the only way to stop their evil ways was to kill them, and felt no remorse at taking Manuel's life.

Which same left Ramon. Badly injured though

he was, with an eye that he would never see through again, the Mexican still drew his gun and started shooting as he made for his horse. Twice he fired and, even though pain misted his eyes, he sent the bullets into the wagon box. Splinters kicked into the air but Calamity's luck, now changed again for the better, held, and the bullets missed her. Yet she knew she must shoot back for Ramon had other charges in his gun and clearly aimed to use them. Her rescuer appeared to judge the situation in the same light for his rifle spat out at the same moment as Calamity's carbine cracked. Struck by two flat-nosed, Tyler Henry-designed .44 bullets, Ramon whirled around twice, crashed into the nearest horse and went down.

Silence dropped after the thunder of guns, the wind wafting away the burned powder's smoke. Calamity let out a long shuddering sigh and lowered her carbine. She felt that the last half hour or so put years on her life and, sure as hell's for sinners, was about as close a call as ever came her young way; up to and including the time she acted as human decoy to lure out of hiding a murderer who had strangled eight girls in the old city of New Orleans. And *that* time had been mighty rough, for she wound up taking the Strangler alone; due partly to her own cussedness and mule-headedly going out without a police cover. She reckoned that not even the feel of the Strangler's killing cord around her throat had been as bad as waiting for those four Mexicans to jump her.

"Are you all right, ma'am?" called a male voice.

For the first time Calamity saw her rescuer. He stepped from the shelter and cover of the bushes some fifty yards away, his rifle held in both hands down before his body yet ready for instant use. Although he wore no badge of office he handled himself in the manner of a trained lawman. Despite calling out the question about her welfare, he never took his attention from the four Mexicans.

Calamity studied her rescuer with interest. There appeared to be something familiar about his features; as if she should know him, yet could not place him. He stood maybe six foot one, with a good pair of shoulders that trimmed down to a lean waist. An expensive black Stetson hat, low crowned and wide brimmed in the Texas fashion, sat on the back of his dusty-blond head. He had an intelligent, handsome face made even more grim-looking by trail dirt and a three-day stubble of whiskers, but it looked like it might relax under the right conditions. The tight rolled green bandana which trailed long ends down over his blue broadcloth shirt, his brown levis pants with the cuffs turned back and hanging outside his high-heeled, fancy-stitched boots, all were trail-dirty and showed hard wear. His gunbelt hung just right, a brace of matched staghorn butted 1860

Army Colts in the contoured holsters. The guns rode just right for a fast draw and in a significant fashion; the right side's Colt pointed its butt to the rear, that at the left turned forward. Such a method often being used in the days before metallic-cartridge revolvers replaced the percussion-fired guns. Due to the slowness of reloading a cap-and-ball revolver, many men carried two guns, although few learned to be ambidextrous in the use of their weapons. Most folks toted their left gun so it could be drawn with the right hand. In a tight spot which called for sustained fire from his weapons, the young man who rescued Calamity most likely drew and emptied his right side Colt first, then either holstered it or made a border-shift—tossing the gun from right to left hand—and drew the second weapon cross-hand so as to continue shooting.

"Dang it though," Calamity mused, studying the young man. "I should know this feller from someplace. Now who in hell does he remind me of?"

Quickly Calamity thought of some of the men who passed through her hectic young life, trying to decide which of them the young Texan reminded her of most. She discounted Wild Bill Hickok right away. Nor did her rescuer remind her of Beau Resin, the Indian scout she met while freighting supplies to a fort in the Dakotas and with whom she shared some mighty stirring times. Her thoughts went next to Mark Counter, that range-country Hercules from the Texas Big Bend country. No, handsome though he was, the young man did not come up to Mark's standards, nor resemble the blond giant enough to remind Calamity of Mark. Yet he for sure looked like somebody Calamity knew.

Even as the girl decided to ask, she saw something that jolted all thoughts of who the young Texan resembled clean out of her head.

"Look out!" she screamed.

Clearly Choya, leader of the *Comancheros,* had not been hit as badly as they imagined. Suddenly, his eyes opened and his right hand scooped up the Remington in a fast-done move. He had been playing possum to lure his unseen attack in close enough to be shot down. The move came fast, deadly and unexpected as the strike of a copperhead snake, and was typical of a *Comanchero's* way of fighting. Even as Choya fired, and almost before Calamity screamed her warning, the young Texan acted. He moved with commendable speed, going into a crouch and lining the rifle hip high. Three times he fired, working the lever in almost a blur of movement. Choya got off one shot which fanned the Texan's cheek in passing and might have hit if the *Comanchero's* hand had been steadier. Twice splinters erupted from the wall, drawing closer to Choya. On the third shot no splinters flew, but the *Comanchero* jerked under the impact of lead. For an instant he struggled to keep his gun lined. The Texan levered another bullet into his rifle and prepared to shoot again. The precaution proved to be unnecessary. Opening his hand, Choya let the Remington fall from it. This time when the gun landed on the ground, Choya would not be picking it up again.

Chapter 4

YOU'RE DUSTY FOG'S KID BROTHER

~~~

"RECKON YOU FEEL UP TO COVERING THEM WHILE I pull their fangs, ma'am?" asked the young man who had saved Calamity's life, his voice an easy-sounding Texas drawl.

Maybe Calamity did feel just a little mite shaken by her experience, but the words stiffened her like a hound-scared cat.

"Naw!" she replied. "I'm all set to start swooning and like to pee my tiny pants." She hefted the carbine for him to see. "Go pull their teeth, friend, they're safe covered."

Watching the way the young man moved, Calamity once again felt struck by the calm, competent and efficient manner in which he handled himself. One thing was for certain sure, he moved like a well-trained lawman. His route to the bodies took him by the front of Calamity's wagon. In passing, he rested the Winchester against the wagon's side and took out his right-hand revolver before going any closer to the dead Mexicans. Up close, should one of the quartet still be playing possum, a revolver's short length licked the bejeesus out of the longer range and greater magazine capacity of a rifle.

Neither weapon would have been needed, as the disarming of the *Comancheros* passed without incident. Not one of that evil quartet would ever give trouble or endanger lives and property again. Yet the young Texan did not feel any annoyance at having taken the precautions. The way he saw things, it was well worth taking a few added precautions happen they kept a man alive.

"That's them cleaned," he remarked, after tossing the last of the *Comancheros'* weapons toward the wagon. "You'd maybe best stop in the wagon, ma'am, they aren't a pretty sight."

"They never are," Calamity answered, putting her carbine's safety catch on and sliding the little gun back into its boot. "And for Tophet's sake, stop calling me 'ma'am'."

"Sure, ma'am," drawled the young man soothingly.

If there was one thing in the world that riled

Calamity more than the rest, it was having a young feller around her age showing off his masculine superiority—not that Calamity would have expressed it in such a manner—and acting all smug and condescending because he wore pants and maybe sported hair on his chest. Well, maybe she might be a mite shy on the hair but she could sure copper his bet on the other score. Unfastening the skirt, she slid it off and, not for the first time, wondered why in hell womenfolk hampered themselves by wearing such garments. Once free of the skirt's encumbrance, she took up her gunbelt and vaulted lightly from the wagon.

"You look a mite disappointed," she said noticing the way he glanced at her legs.

"Why sure," the Texan replied. "When I saw you take off your skirt there, I figured——"

"Well, you was wrong. Let's clean up around here afore the Jones' get back."

"As you say, ma'am. This isn't your place then?"

"Just passing through, although I did take a few liberties with the fixings," Calamity answered, her eyes flickering to the window she destroyed in her departure from the cabin. "And the next time you call me 'ma'am' I'll——"

"Ma'am's a good name seeing's we've not been introduced. I figured you was a lady in distress."

"Boy," grinned Calamity, although her rescuer could maybe give her a year in age. "I'm no lady, but I sure as hell was in distress. Fact being I was so in distress that I said, 'Calam, gal,' I said, 'you're sure in distress right now, so where-at's that long, blond, handsome Texan who's going to save your ornery, worthless lady's hide.' And dog-my-cats, there you was as large as life and twice as welcome."

"I talk too much when I want to haul off and fetch up, too," the Texan told her. "Like right now."

For a moment Calamity's temper boiled up hot and wild, quelling the uneasiness in her belly. No matter how often one saw sudden death, the sight never grew any easier on the stomach. Those four Mexicans aimed to rape and kill her, as she well knew, but the thought did little to stop her feeling just a mite sick as she glanced at, then looked away from the gory mess that was the top of Gomez' bullet-shattered head.

However, life must go on. If Calamity sat down and went all woman and hysterical every time she saw a body, she would have spent a good portion of the last three years that way. A freight driver's life was hard and dangerous out West, what with facing the hazards of the elements, Indian attack and the occasional meeting with murderous *Comancheros,* so offered plenty of opportunity for one to see sudden, violent death.

After her mother left her in the care of the nuns

at a St. Louis convent, Calamity stayed put until her sixteenth birthday. There being too much of Charlotte Canary's spirit in Calamity for her to take kindly to the discipline of the convent, the girl slipped away on her sixteenth birthday and hid in one of Dobe Killem's wagons as it started its trip West, first working as cook's louse, then learning the mysteries of a team-driver's art. From the men of the outfit Calamity learned much; how to handle and care for a six-horse team, use a long-lashed bull whip as tool and weapon, know more than a little about Indians, and how to defend herself with her bare hands in a rough-house frontier barroom brawl—a useful accomplishment when dealing with tough dancehall girls who objected to Calamity entering their place of employment. In three years Calamity had seen a fair piece of the West and reached the stage of competence where Dobe Killem allowed her to handle chores alone, knowing he could trust her to come through for him.

"What'll we do with 'em?" she asked, ignoring the unsettled condition of her stomach. "It'll take a whole heap of digging to plant all four of 'em; and I don't want to do it near the house."

"We won't have to," answered the Texan. "If you've room in your wagon, I'll take them into Austin."

"You a bounty hunter?" growled Calamity.

Reaching into a hidden pocket behind his gun-belt, the Texan extracted something. He held out his hand, in its palm lay a silver star mounted in a circle. While not a native of the Lone Star State, Calamity still knew and could recognize the badge of the Texas Rangers when she saw it—and she saw one in the palm of her young rescuer's hand.

"Ranger, huh?" she asked.

"Yes'm. The name's Danny Fog——"

Calamity slapped the palm of a hand against her thigh and gave an exasperated yelp. Everything slotted into place now, she could see the family resemblance and cursed herself for not spotting it straight off. Of course, there was a mite of difference that could account for her not connecting her rescuer with——

"Damn it to hell!" she snorted. "I should have seen it. You're Dusty Fog's kid brother."

Which same was roughly the sort of remark Danny Fog had come to expect to hear when he announced his identity. Danny yielded second to no man in the respect, admiration and affection he bore for his famous brother, the Rio Hondo gun wizard, Dusty Fog. As Danny saw things, a man who had been one of the South's top fighting leaders in the war, became known as a cowhand, ranch segundo and trail boss of the first water, bore a name as a town-taming lawman with few equals, was acclaimed by reliable sources as the fastest gun in Texas, deserved all the credit and fame which came his way. So far Texas had not come under the grip of "debunkers," those intellectual young men who, aware of their own complete lack of any qualities of courage or ability, sought to bring everybody down to their level. Dusty Fog enjoyed just fame and acclaim and his brother, Danny, stood first in line to give it.

But it sure riled a mite to be known as "Dusty Fog's kid brother." Without boasting of it, Danny knew himself to be intelligent; with his training he considered himself to be a pretty fair lawman; maybe not *real* fast with a Colt—it took him a good second to draw and shoot and in Texas one needed to be able to almost half that time to be considered fast—but a fine shot with a handgun or rifle; capable of reading sign in an efficient manner, and a reckonable fist fighter; these latter qualities stemming from the lessons given by two of Dusty's friends, each an acknowledged master in his field. So he figured he could make a better than fair peace officer, given time to gather experience and reckoned he ought to be able to stand on his own two feet; which was why he joined the Rangers instead of staying on in Rio Hondo County and working as his father's deputy. That way he hoped to gain for himself a separate identity instead of living as "Dusty Fog's kid brother."

"You know Dusty, ma'am?" he inquired.

With a remarkable show of tact, Calamity guessed at the cause of the momentary pause which followed her words. So she held down the blistering comment which rose on Danny's repeated use of the word "ma'am."

"Met him a couple of times, and the Ysabel Kid—know ole Mark Counter a whole heap better though. Say, didn't they ever mention me?"

"Only gal they ever mentioned that partly might fit your description was a dead-mean, red-haired lump of perversity called Calamity Jane. Only Mark mentioned as how she was a mite fatter'n you and got more freckles."

"If you're jobbing me——" she warned.

"Me, ma'am?" asked Danny, then a look of horror came to his face. "Landsakes a-mercy, do you mean to tell me that *you're* Calamity Jane?"

"You did that real smooth," Calamity sniffed. "Maybe just a mite over-done, but not bad for a kid."

A grin flickered on Danny's face and he held out a hand. "Put her there, Calam. Pleased to know you."

Taking the offered hand, Calamity shook it and grinned back. "And boy, was I pleased to hear from you. Say, let's tend to the cleaning up afore we set down to old home week, shall we?"

"Be best, I reckon," Danny agreed. "Can we tote 'em in on your wagon?"

"Reckon so. I never took to handling the blister end of a shovel."

"I'll go bring down my hoss first."

"Reckon I'll come along with you," Calamity remarked, throwing a glance at the bodies. "Feel like stretching my legs a mite."

"Let's go then," Danny answered.

He made no comment on the girl's statement, although she figured that her words had not fooled him at all. Side by side they started to walk up the bush dotted slope and Calamity's curiosity got the better of her as she thought of Danny's timely arrival.

"How'd you come to be on hand right when I needed you?" she asked.

"I've been after Choya and his bunch for over a week now."

"Just one of you?"

"Were three when we started out. Only the *Comancheros* laid for us. Got Buck Lemming, him being the sergeant, first crack and put lead into Sandy Gartree's left wing. I was riding behind the other two and come off lucky. Then when Choya's bunch pulled a Mexican stand-off. I buried Buck, patched up Sandy and sent him back to the Bradded H and took out to tracking those four."

Which left a considerable amount of the story untold. Danny spoke truly when he said he had been riding behind the other two as they ran into the ambush. What he failed to mention being that he saved Gartree's life by pulling the wounded man to cover under *Comanchero* fire and it had been mainly due to his defense that the four remaining Mexicans—two died before Danny and Gartree's guns—pulled out and ran. In the traditions of the Texas Rangers, Danny attended to his friends and then took out after the *Comancheros* even though the odds be four to one in their favor.

"Sure pleased you did," Calamity stated. "Man, there was times when I figured I was due for wings and a harp."

"*You*. Shucks, only the good die young they do say," grinned Danny.

"One more remark like that out of you and we'll see about it," she snorted. "What was you fixing in to do, sneaking down the slope?"

"Take 'em. I'd seen their hosses when they jumped us and recognized those four when I peeked over the top of the rim. Reckoned that Choya and his bunch'd be in the house and aimed to sneak in then take 'em by surprise. Only you come through the window afore I made it. Which same I was lucky, didn't know about that jasper in the backhouse."

"The Ysabel Kid'd've checked on it afore *he* moved in."

"Which same I aimed to do," Danny told her calmly. "He taught me all he knows about tracking and things."

"Which same I never saw the Kid show any sign of knowing about—things," grinned Calamity. "Though he does know some about tracking."

"Anyways you stopped me when you came through the window and that jasper came out the backhouse like a coon off a log when he heard the whooping and hollering, and I figured to stay hid until I saw what might be needed. How come you-all was fool enough to get caught, Calam, gal?"

Quickly, her sentences liberally sprinkled with a flow of invective that brought an admiring grin to Danny's lips, Calamity told her story. Nor did his admiration lessen when he heard of the manner in which she prevented the men from recognizing her true potential by donning a skirt and acting as the unsuspecting lady of the house. Take it any way a man looked, old Calamity was quite a gal and lived up to the flattering comments Dusty, Mark and the Kid made about her after their return from the first meeting. Not many women would have shown her presence of mind. Fact being, few women, even in the self-reliant West, could have handled things so efficiently or come out of the situation which had faced Calamity as well as she did.

On reaching the top of the slope, Calamity looked to where Danny's horse stood by a large blueberry bush. It came as almost a surprise to see that Danny did not ride a paint like his brother's personal mount. However, the horse looked to be a real fine critter, sixteen hands high and showing good breeding. The horse had a coloration Calamity could never remember seeing before, a light red, almost pinkish roan with a pure white belly.

"What in hell color do you call that?" she asked.

"A *sabino*," Danny explained. "Got him below the line. Mexican cowhands go a whole heap on them for go-to-town hosses and for work."

"I'll take your word for it," sniffed Calamity. "Looks a mite flashy to me. Got me a buckskin with the outfit that'd run his legs down to the shoulders in a straight mile race."

"Got me a week's furlough to come when I pull in from this lot," Danny answered, meeting her challenge. "Happen you can lay hands on your crow-bait, we'll run us a race."

"You got a deal. Dobe Killem, which same being my boss, told me to wait in Austin for two weeks, grab some work if I could to keep me busy until he brings the rest of the bunch in."

"So you'll be in for a week with nothing to do," drawled Danny, taking up his *sabino's* reins. "Just like me."

"Must be fate in it someplace." Calamity answered, eyeing him with interest. "You got a steady gal?"

"Not steady. Always figgered a young lawman shouldn't get too close or attached until he knows if he's going to make the grade or not."

"Which same's as good an excuse as any."

"Sure," Danny agreed. "Now let's get down there and tend to those four Mexicans, shall we?"

"I thought you'd never ask," Calamity answered.

On returning to the cabin, Danny attended to his horse. Then, with Calamity at his side, he returned to the front of the cabin and prepared to start the distasteful task of cleaning up.

"Get their tarps, Calam," he ordered, "and bring one of their ropes."

Normally Calamity might have objected to a new acquaintance, especially a young man, giving her orders. Yet she figured Danny knew what he was doing, and anyways she could always object if she decided he did not. Calamity went to each horse in turn and removed its tarpaulin-wrapped bundle from behind the saddle's cantle. Unrolling the first bundle, she handed the tarp to Danny and, with an express of distaste on his face, he went to work. First spreading the tarp on the ground, Danny pulled Choya's body into the center of it. Wrapping the body completely inside the tarp, Danny took the rope from Calamity and bound the bundle so the jolting of the wagon would not uncover its grisly contents. Next came a difficult and not too pleasant task, loading the body into the rear of Calamity's wagon.

"I'll lend you a hand," the girl said her voice just a mite strained.

"*Gracias,* Calam. Take the feet, I'll handle the head."

Between them, Calamity and Danny lifted first one, then the remainder of the tarpaulin-wrapped shapes into the rear of the girl's wagon, laying them side by side in the space at the back. With that done, the two of them cleaned up, as well as they could, the traces of the fighting. Calamity gathered up the shattered glass while Danny brought shovel-loads of dirt to cover the blood-stains. Finally they stood back and looked over their work.

"I took a bath when I arrived," the girl remarked. "Damned if I don't feel all dirty again."

Danny put a hand to his bristle-covered chin. "And me. I sure hate to have whiskers growing on me. Say, is there any water inside?"

"I'll boil some for you. Then while you're shaving, I'll go take a bath," Calamity suggested. "And then I'll cook us a meal."

"Sounds like a real good notion," Danny answered.

Opening his bedroll, Danny dug into his warbag and collected his shaving kit. Calamity poured him out some hot water and headed for the swimming hole while he stripped off his shirt to wash and shave. Having been hunting the *Comancheros* alone for the past three days, Danny had not found time to wash and shave, or even take off his clothes. He felt a whole heap better with the growth of whiskers and some of the trail dirt removed from his hide. On Calamity's return, Danny took a change of clothes and headed for the swimming hole. All in all, he both felt and looked a whole heap better on his return. Nor had Calamity wasted her time, but set to and cooked a real good meal for him.

"You cook just like Mark said," he told Calamity after the meal, having been too hungry during it to waste time in talking. "Man gets tired of stream water and jerky."

"Reckon he does," she agreed then grinned. "You mean ole Mark said something nice about me?"

"Shucks, Mark always talks real high and respectful about you, Calam."

"I just bet he does," smiled the girl.

"There's no chance of making Austin today," Danny remarked, looking out of the window at the darkening range. "Happen we start at sun-up, we ought to reach it afore noon tomorrow."

"That's how I saw it," agreed Calamity. "Let's go tend the stock. I reckon we'll leave the four *Comanchero* hosses here to pay for the damage I did to the window."

Danny gave his assent and they went out to feed, water and bed down the horses. On their return, Calamity lit a lamp while Danny laid his saddle carefully on its side by the wall and unpacked his bedroll.

"It's going to be a mite chilly for whoever sleeps in here," Calamity said, glancing at the shattered window.

"You take the bedroom then," replied Danny, courteous to the core as became a Southern gentleman.

"Shuckens no. Let's do it fair," answered Calamity, taking a coin from her pocket and flipping it into the air. "Heads I have the bedroom, tails you get it. Dang it, Danny, it's tails. We said best of three, didn't we?"

"Why sure," grinned Danny, taking the coin and flicking it up again. It landed on the table with a metallic clink.

"Three out of five, we said, didn't we?" asked Calamity, looking at the exposed tails side.

Once more the coin sailed into the air. Shooting out a hand, Calamity caught the spinning disc of metal and brought it down to stand on its edge in a crack on the table top.

"Land-sakes a-mercy," she said innocently. "It looks like we're due for a stand-off."

"What'll we do in that case?" asked Danny, just as innocently.

"Didn't Mark teach you nothing about—things?"

"You know, Calam, gal," Danny drawled, blowing out the lamp. "He just might have done at that."

Almost an hour later, just before she went to sleep, Calamity gave a grin. One thing was for sure. Dusty Fog's kid brother could sure act like a man full grown.

Chapter 5

BREAK UP THAT COW STEALING, DANNY

SID WATCHHORN EASED HIS ARM IN THE SLING, glanced at the rider and wagon which entered the compound and then walked back into the office.

"Danny's here, Cap'n," he said.

"Alone?" asked Murat, seeing his chance of making the Caspar County investigation—and getting away from the tedium of office work—depart.

"Never thought he'd bring any of 'em in alive," Sid answered. "Only he's not alone. Got a right pretty lil gal along with him, driving a six-hoss Conestoga."

Throwing a glance at Sid, the Ranger captain tried to read the tanned, leathery face for a hint that his wounded man made a joke. He saw nothing, which did not entirely surprise him. However, Murat knew handling the ribbons of a *six*-horse Conestoga wagon took skill of a high degree. Coming to his feet, Murat walked from the office and looked in the direction of the approaching party.

"I told you so," said Sid in doleful delight, "only you didn't believe lil ole me."

"Does anybody?" grunted Murat and walked to meet his other Ranger. "Howdy, Danny. We got a telegraph from Sandy up to Two Trees, said you'd gone on after Choya and his bunch."

"Huh huh!" Danny answered.

"Catch 'em?"

The words came out more as a statement than a question. No Ranger worth his salt would leave the trail of the men who killed one of his partners and wounded another. Yet Murat could see no sign of the *Comanchero's* horses. Then his eyes went to the wagon's box, studying the various scars on its timber. Two of the bullet holes looked newly made.

"I caught 'em. They're in the back of Calam's wagon."

Walking by his captain, Sid headed to the rear of the wagon and started to unfasten its canopy's lashings. Calamity jumped down from the box and joined the Ranger at the rear.

"Let me lend you a hand," she said. "You look like you need one."

"Her husband come home early," answered Sid.

"That's allus the way," Calamity commiserated.

"How many in there, ma'am?"

"Four, all there was. And happen you don't want the other wing busting quit calling me 'ma'am'."

One of the young wranglers dashed up and took charge of Danny's horse. It said much for Danny's trust in the youngster that he allowed the *sabino's* welfare to the boy's hands. However, Danny knew he could rely on the youngster to care properly for the big horse and that he must give his report to his captain as quickly as possible.

"Let's go into the office, Danny," Murat suggested as the youngster led the *sabino* away.

Following Murat into the office, Danny took a seat at the desk. There was nothing fancy about the room in which the Rangers of Company "G" handled their paper-work and planned their campaigns against the criminal elements of Texas. Just a desk, its top scarred by spur-decorated boot heels and burned by innumerable cigar and cigarette butts, with a few papers sharing the top with the first edition of the famous "Bible Two," the Texas Rangers' list of wanted men that would be brought out each year and read by the sons of the star-in-the-circle far more than they ever studied the original book. Some half-a-dozen chairs stood against the walls, two more at the desk. A safe, its door open and shelves empty, graced one wall, a stove facing it across the room. On either side of the door leading to the cells at the rear of the building were respectively a bulletin board containing wanted dodgers from all over the State, and a rack holding some dozen assorted Winchesters, Spencer carbines and ten-gauge shotguns, all clean and ready for use.

It was not a room conducive to long, leisurely discussion, but a plain, functioning, working-man's premises where business was dealt with speedily and without waste of time.

"Tell me about it," Murat ordered as they took their seats. He took out the office bottle and poured two drinks, offered the young Ranger a cigar, and settled down to learn how Danny handled things on the hunt for the *Comancheros*.

A feeling of pride came to Danny as he took the drink. It had become a custom in Company "G" that Murat offered a Ranger who came in from a successful chore a drink before starting business. Usually it would have been the senior man making the report and collecting the drink, but this time— for the first time—Danny found himself receiving Murat's unspoken approbation.

Quickly Danny told Murat all that happened from the time the *Comancheros* ambushed his party. By questions; knowing his men, Murat never expected to learn the one making the report's share of the affair without probing; the captain found out how Danny handled things with his sergeant dead and more experienced colleague wounded. Nodding in approval, he listened to Danny tell how the trailing of the *Comancheros* came to its conclusion at the Jones place. The captain's eyebrows lifted slightly as he learned the identity of the girl on the wagon. It figured, happen a man gave thought to the matter; few other women in the West could handle a six-horse Conestoga wagon.

"Four, and the two you downed when they hit you," Murat said when Danny came to the end of his report. "That's the whole damned bunch finished."

"And it cost us Buck Lemming," Danny replied. "He was married, got a family, too, Captain."

"I know that," answered Murat. "It's the way the game goes, Danny."

"If I'd been up front——"

"Call *that* right off, boy!" the captain snapped. "Buck rode up front because it was his place as sergeant to be there. Nobody'll blame you for the ambush, and what you've done since sure don't need any apologizing for. Well, we can scratch Choya's name out of 'Bible Two'."

"Yes, sir. Anything more for me?"

"Yep. I want you to pull out for Caspar, today, if you can."

"Something up?"

"Cow thieves."

Danny looked at the commander of Company "G" and nodded. A Ranger never knew from one day to the next what new trouble he might find himself tangling in. Fresh off the trail of a band of murderous *Comancheros,* he found himself detailed to ride out the same night to deal with a bunch of cow thieves—even if his captain had not said it in so many words.

"Sounds a mite urgent just for cow thieves," Danny remarked, knowing such business was mostly handled by the county authorities concerned and did not normally require the Statewide powers of the Rangers.

"It goes deeper than that," answered Murat and settled down to explain the situation to Danny, including the possibility of far worse trouble than mere cow stealing developing out of the hiring of professional gun hands. Then Murat told Danny the most prime piece of information.

"A woman running it?" Danny growled. "That doesn't sound possible."

"Neither does seeing a gal handle the ribbons of a six-horse Conestoga—only we've both just seen *that*. Anyways, she has a perfect set-up to run it. A saloon where cowhands can come and go without attracting any attention; things even a saint* likes enough to make him think about grabbing a cou-

---

* Saint: Cow thief's contemptuous name for a loyal cowhand.

ple of unbranded strays, working on them with a running iron and selling them to pay for."

"That figgers," agreed Danny. "Most young cowhands'd take a few chances to get extra liquor, gambling or gals. Only a gal running things makes it just that much harder."

"It sure does."

Studying Danny, Murat wondered if the task might be beyond the inexperienced young man's depth. Sure Danny had trailed and downed that bunch of *Comancheros* without calling for help, but that had been a straightforward piece of work. Tangling with the cow thieves and gathering evidence against their leaders, called for courage, brains—which Murat granted Danny possessed—and experience. It was the latter Danny fell short on. Yet he might be a good man for the job. At least he would be the right age for Ella Watson, or whoever controlled the stealing, to regard as a potential cow thief, and he knew enough about cowhand work to act the part without arousing suspicion.

But could Danny swing things up there in Caspar and prevent another range war blowing a further Texas county apart at the seams?

Then Murat remembered Danny's relationship with Dusty Fog. Should Danny find himself in water over the willows up in Caspar County, a word would bring his famous brother riding to his aid. Nor would Dusty ride alone, but bring along his two good and efficient *amigos* Mark Counter and the Ysabel Kid. While none of that illustrious trio had ever belonged to the Rangers, they could handle the trouble in Caspar County with ease.

While rolling a cigarette, Danny watched Murat and guessed at his captain's thoughts. His knowledge did not annoy him as much as it might have done before taking the *Comanchero* gang. Now he had proved himself in his own eyes and one thing he knew for sure. Should he handle the Caspar chore, no matter how difficult the task or how it went, he did not aim to call on Brother Dusty for help. Danny reckoned that if he could not stand on his own two feet by now, he was of no use as a Ranger.

Only having a woman at the back of the business surely made it hellish hard to handle. Danny had decided on the same line of action as that thought out by Murat. Going into Caspar as a drifting cowhand, taking on at a ranch and then letting himself be drawn into the cow stealing, seemed like the quickest way to learn who stood behind the business. Catching the actual thieves would be easy enough that way; but, from what the captain said, they were only dupes. It was the brains behind the stealing Danny wanted. One did not kill a snake by cutting off its rattles, but by stamping on its head. Remove the dupes and the organizer would lie low for a time, then emerge and corrupt another bunch of fool young cowhands, turn them from honest, loyal hands to thieves.

"Reckon you can handle it, Danny?" asked Murat. "You can go in any way you want. I won't hold you back."

"I reckon I can," Danny agreed.

At that moment the office door opened to admit Calamity and Sid.

"We've took the bodies down to the undertaker, Cap'n," said the Ranger. "I reckoned you might like to have a jaw with Calamity, so she left her wagon at Smith's store to be unloaded and come back with me."

"Take a seat, Calamity," Murat said, rising. "Could I offer you a drink?"

"Just a teensie-weensie lil three fingers," she answered, accepting the chair Danny drew up for her. "Wouldn't say no to one of them fancy cigars, neither."

With any other woman, the request might have appeared as an affectation. Yet somehow the sight of Calamity seated with a foot raised on the desk, puffing appreciatively at one of Murat's thin, crooked black cigars, looked entirely natural.

"I'd like to thank you officially for helping Danny get the *Comancheros,*" Murat told the girl.

"Shuckens, he helped me more than I helped him. Anyways, to pay me back he promised to show me the sights of Austin City."

"You done seen me, gal," Sid remarked. "Ain't no other sights worth seeing."

"Leave us not forget Calamity's a visitor to Texas, Sid," Murat growled. "Don't make her retch. Anyways, when was this sightseeing to be done?"

"Starting tonight."

"Only he'll be riding out this evening."

Calamity's eyes went to Danny, then back and met Murat's. "Must be something real urgent, Cap'n."

"Urgent enough," agreed Murat, studying the girl and remembering all the stories he had heard about her. Maybe some of them were a mite lengthened, but from the way she handled her end of the *Comanchero* business, she had sand to burn and did not spook when the going became rough. Slowly Murat swung his eyes to Danny and read mutual thoughts on the subject of Calamity in the young Ranger's mind. Murat almost gave in, then shook his head. "No. It just couldn't be done."

"If I knew what the hell you meant, I'd agree," Calamity answered.

"I don't see why it couldn't," Danny put in. "Calamity's got two weeks at least to hang around Austin afore her boss gets here."

"Just what are you pair——" Calamity began.

"It'd be too dangerous, Danny."

"That gal eats danger, Cap'n."

"Hey! What the blue-blistering hell——"

"She might not care for the idea."

"Why not put it to her, Cap'n?" asked Sid, enjoying watching the expressions on Calamity's face while the conversation went on.

"Hold it! Hold IT!" she suddenly yelled, pounding a hand on the table top. "Just dig in your tiny Texas feet and let a half-smart lil Northern gal catch up with you."

"Huh—Oh, hi there, Calam," Danny drawled. "Plumb forgot you was here."

The girl replied in a hide blistering flow of invective which drew admiring grins from the listening men. Throughout the flow Sid listened spell-bound and at its conclusion could barely hold down his applause for a mighty fine demonstration of the ancient and honorable art of cussing.

"How about it, Sid?" asked Murat. "Will she do?"

"Don't know what for, Cap'n, but it sounds like you want me to say 'yes,' so being good, loyal and wanting an advance on next month's pay, I'll say it. Yes, I reckon she'll do right well."

"And me," Danny agreed.

Clapping a hand to her forehead, Calamity gave a groan. "My mammy never gave me much advice, but she always told me to stay clear of Texas and Texans. When I first met Mark Counter I figgered she was right. But getting to know you three's changed my mind."

"Has, huh?" asked Danny sympathetically.

"It sure as hell has!" Calamity yelped. "Now I *know* she was right."

"To get serious, Calam,"·Murat put in, "how'd you like to help us?"

"How'd you mean, help you?" she asked suspiciously.

"We've something on that needs a woman's gentle touch."

"It's nothing to do with some gals getting strangled, is it?"

"No," answered Murat, sounding a mite startled. "Why should it be?"

"No reason at all, 'cepting that the last time a lawman said something like that to me, I near on wound up getting choked by a murdering skunk. Enjoyed it so much that I figured I'd like a second go."

"Happen they get on to you, if you take the chore, you'll likely get your wanting," Murat stated and explained his idea to Calamity.

When Murat finished speaking, Calamity looked him over with interested eyes. It appeared that the situation was not as dangerous as she first imagined. No sir, it was even worse. With a rope waiting on their capture, cow thieves tended to be a mite rough should they find a spy in their midst. If she went in to Caspar, she would not have the cover of police escort as she had, until the final night—when, to be fair, she ought not to have gone out—in New Orleans. However, Calamity reckoned she might be able to take good care of herself, especially against another woman; after all no gal had ever licked her yet.

"You'll not be able to go into the saloon dressed like that, Calam," Danny pointed out.

"Now me, I'd swear every saloon gal dressed this way," she sniffed.

"We can easy fix the clothes," Murat went on.

"Yeah," groaned the girl. "I figured you might. I can't stay on for long though. Dobe Killem wants me back with the outfit when he pulls out of here."

"If you haven't got us the proof we need in nine or ten days, you likely won't get it at all," Murat replied. "How about it, Calam?"

"You just hired yourself a gal," she answered, holding out her hand. "When do we start, Danny?"

"Now slow down a mite, gal," Murat ordered. "It's not as easy as all that."

"Happen I'd thought it would be, I'd never have taken on," Calamity told him calmly.

Despite her eagerness to try the novel experience of working as a saloon-girl and undercover agent for the Texas Rangers, Calamity knew nothing must be left to chance. She found Murat's preparations remarkably, and comfortingly from her point of view, thorough. Knowing that certain and painful death awaited Calamity if she should be detected as a spy, Murat intended that she should take as few chances as possible. While Danny Fog would also be working in Caspar County, he could not be on hand all the time to protect Calamity. Mostly the girl would have to stand on her own two feet and rely on her brains, courage and ability.

Collecting a trio of horses from the remuda, Calamity, Danny and Murat rode into Austin. During the trip, Murat gave Danny and Calamity instructions. Danny was to take the name Daniel Forgrave, a cowhand who had worked on three different ranches well clear of the Caspar area. Making sure Danny could remember the names of the outfits and their bosses, Murat turned his attention to Calamity. After some discussion they settled on the name Martha Connelly for her and once more Murat gave a list of places where she had worked.

"Remember those four, whatever you do," Murat warned.

"What if somebody knows them?" she countered.

"That's always a chance, Calam," admitted the Ranger captain. "You can always pull out. Fact being, you'd be wise if you did."

"Never was wise," she grinned. "You reckon it's a good thing to use the Golden Slipper here in town, they could right easy telegraph here and ask about me."

"You'll be all right, even if they do," Murat promised.

While Calamity trusted Murat's judgment, she figured out one detail that a man would be unlikely to think about. She expected to be taken to some dress shop and fitted with clothing suitable for her pose as a saloon-girl and saw danger in the idea. Then she discovered that Murat had been aware of the problem of dress and knew the answer to it.

Instead of visiting a dress shop, Calamity found herself taken in the rear of the Golden Slipper, one of Austin's better class saloons. Clearly Murat knew his way around the place, for he led his party upstairs to the office of the owner, a big, buxom, jovial woman who greeted him as a friend and lent a sympathetic, understanding ear to the problems facing the Ranger captain.

"Nothing easier, Jules," she stated after hearing what Murat required. "You boys go downstairs and have a drink on the house while I fix up Calamity with all she'll need."

Half an hour later Calamity entered the bar-room, only she looked a whole heap different from the girl who came to town with Danny. Gone were the men's clothing, gunbelt and bull-whip, replaced by a small, dainty and impractical hat, a dress with black and white candy-striped bodice and mauve skirt, some cheap, flashy jewellery and a reticule, such as a saloon-girl would wear when travelling. None of the items were new, but had been selected from clothing left behind by girls who departed into the respectability of married life.

Calamity had figured suspicion might come her way should she show up in Caspar with every item of clothing damned near brand new. However, Murat appeared to have foreseen the danger and countered it by arranging for her to loan a wardrobe suited to the part she was going to play.

"Got all you need, Calamity?" the captain asked as the girl joined him and Danny at their table.

"Just about all," she replied. "Got me this out-fit, three fancy saloon gal frocks, shoes, stockings and some fancy female do-dads you pair don't know the name of, or ought to be ashamed of yourselves if you do. Ain't but one thing more I'd like along with me."

"And what's that?" asked Danny.

"One of those forty-one caliber Remington belly guns."

Such an item would not arouse suspicion, or be out of place in a saloon-girl's possession. Many a girl working in a saloon or dancehall carried a Remington Double Derringer, or some other such small, easily concealed firearm, in her reticule, or strapped to her garter.

"There's one in my office and some shells for it," Murat told the girl. "I can let you have it as soon as we've bought your stage ticket to Caspar. You'll go on tomorrow's stage and be there in three days."

"I'll pull out now," Danny drawled. "That should see me in town a day ahead of Calamity."

"Reckon it should," agreed Murat. "Break up that cow stealing, Danny."

"Yes, sir, Captain," replied Danny soberly. "I aim to do just that."

Chapter 6

LOOKS LIKE I GOT HERE TOO LATE

~~

A PAIR OF SPIRALING TURKEY VULTURES CAUGHT
Danny Fog's eye and caused him to bring his big
sabino to a halt. The sight of those black-plumed
scavengers hovering in the sky never struck a
western man as being a beautiful sight. When
turkey vultures gathered, they followed death
and a corpse, or something near to it, lay below
them. Human or animal, it made no never mind
to a hungry turkey vulture. Gliding down from
the skies, the birds tore flesh from bones and
leaving only a picked skeleton behind when they
departed.

Two days had passed since Danny rode out of
Austin and at almost noon, he figured he must be

on the eastern ranges of Caspar County, most likely crossing Buck Jerome's Bench J.

"Might be nothing, hoss," he said, patting the *sabino's* neck and glancing at the dun cutting horse borrowed from Sid Watchhorn to aid his disguise and which now followed the *sabino* without fighting the rope connecting to Danny's saddle. "I reckon we'd best take us a look though."

Such an action would be in keeping with the character he must play while in Caspar just as much as when he rode in his official capacity of Texas Ranger. Any man seeing circling buzzards—as the non-zoologically-minded Western folk called *Cathartes Aura,* the American turkey vulture—would investigate. The attraction might be either an injured man or animal, or some critter died of a highly infectious disease. In which cases the knowledge could be useful: in the first to save a life; in the second, one might prevent a spread of the infection by prompt action.

From the look of things, the birds circled over a large cottonwood that spread its branches over the range maybe a mile from where Danny sat his horse. A touch of his heels against the *sabino's* flanks started the horse moving and the dun followed it without any fuss. As yet Danny could see nothing of the dead or dying creature which caused the turkey vultures to gather in the sky.

Danny had covered about half a mile when a

bunch of pronghorn antelope burst out of a hollow ahead of him. Stopping the *sabino,* he watched the animals speed away, covering the range at a pace only a very good horse could hope to equal. While Danny loved hunting, and lived in an age when game-preservation had never been heard of, he made no attempt to draw his rifle and cut down any of the fleeing antelope. He carried food in his bedroll and would likely be on some ranch's payroll before it ran out. So there did not appear to be any point in killing a pronghorn and he had never seen any sense in shooting some creature just to see it fall.

Led by a buck that carried a pair of horns which would have gladdened any trophy-hunter's heart, the herd held bunched together and went bounding through the bushes at Danny's right, disappearing into a basin. Just as Danny started the *sabino* moving again, he saw the pronghorns bursting wildly through the bushes, scattering in panic as they raced out of the basin once more.

"Now what in hell did that?" he mused and drew his rifle.

Four possible answers sprang to mind: a bunch of wolves denning up among the bushes; a mountain lion that had been cut off from timber country by the coming of daylight and took what cover it could find: a grizzly or black bear hunting berries, but willing to augment its diet by the flesh of a succulent pronghorn; or the presence of hidden men. Predators all, any one of them would cause such panic among the pronghorns should the fast-moving animals come unexpectedly upon it in the bushes when already fleeing from danger.

Danny nudged his *sabino's* ribs and started the horse moving forward. On reaching the edge of the bushes, he halted the horse and slid from the saddle. Not even as steady an animal as the big *sabino* would face the sudden appearance of one of the predators in thick bush and Danny could think of a number of more pleasant ways to die than under the teeth and claws of a startled grizzly after being pitched from the back of a bear-spooked horse. Of course, there might not be a bear in the bushes, but it cost nothing to take precautions.

Leaving the horses standing, the *sabino's* trailing before it in a manner which it had been trained to regard as holding it still as effectively as if being tied, Danny went into the bushes with some caution. He saw nothing to disturb him or explain the panic among the pronghorns. A flock of scarlet-plumed red cardinal birds lifted from among the bushes at his approach, but nothing dangerous or menacing made its appearance. Ahead of him the bushes opened into a clearing at the bottom of the basin. Danny came to a halt and studied the scene before him with worried, calculating eyes.

"Looks like I got here too late," he thought.

Two bodies lay alongside a dead fire's ashes. Cowhands, Danny concluded from their dress; and of the kind he had ridden from Austin to hunt down if the pair of running irons meant anything. Cautiously he studied the clearing, noting the pair of cow horses which stood tied to the bushes at the far side, then taking in the scene around the fire once more. Moving closer, he looked down at the bodies. One had been shot in the back and must have died without even knowing what hit him. Nor would the second have been given much better chance to defend himself by all appearances. Kneeling by the body, Danny examined the holster and doubted if anything remotely like a fast draw could be made from it. The revolver still lay in the holster, its owner having died before he could draw it.

Cold anger filled Danny as he looked down at the two bodies. Neither cowhand looked to be much gone out of his teens and, ignoring the distortion pain had put on the features, appeared to be normal, pleasant youngsters. These were no hardened criminals, or he missed his guess; only a couple of foolhardy youngsters who acted without thinking. They deserved better than to be shot down like dogs.

Danny was no dreamy-eyed moralist or bigoted intellectual regarding every criminal as a misunderstood victim of society to be molly-coddled and pampered as a warning that crime did not pay. In most cases a man became a criminal because of a disinclination to work and had no intention of changing his ways. As a peace officer and a sensible, thinking man, Danny approved of stiff punishment, up to and including hanging, for habitual criminals. While any form of punishment would be most unlikely to change such a man's ways, it served to deter others from following the criminal's footsteps.

For all his thoughts on the subject, Danny hated to think of the way the two young men died. He promised himself that their killer would pay for the deed.

Throwing aside his feelings, Danny forced himself to think as a lawman and to learn all he could about the happenings of the previous night. Carefully, he studied the ground around him, using the knowledge handed on by that master trailer, the Ysabel Kid. From what he saw, there had been three cow thieves present, all occupied with their illegal business when death struck. The third member of the trio made good his escape, or at least got clear of the fire, for Danny found signs of somebody, possibly the killer, racing a horse across the clearing in the direction taken by the fleeing cow thief.

At that point of the proceedings Danny began to feel puzzled. His examination of the tracks told him that one rider had returned, set free some of the calves and led off three more. Yet the same person did not free the dead men's horses, nor even go near the bodies.

"Sure puzzling," he mused, turning to leave the clearing and return to his horses. "From all I've heard, this looks like Gooch's work. He never takes chances and wouldn't give those boys chance to surrender or make a fight. But why would Gooch free half the calves and take the others. And why would he leave the two bodies when they'd fetch a damned sight more bounty than three calves would bring him?"

A possible answer occurred to Danny as he reached the horses. He stood on Bench J, not Forked C land, so it was not the range Gooch had been hired to protect and the bounty hunter did not work for the love of his labor. Of course, it might not be Gooch who killed the cowhands, although everything pointed in that direction. Most men, especially ranchers and honest cowhands, hated a cow thief, but few would go to the extreme of shooting down two in cold blood. No, it appeared the thing Governor Howard and Captain Murat feared had happened. Tired of merely earning his pay, Gooch left the Forked C range to hunt bounty on other property.

Just as Danny swung into the *sabino's* saddle, a distant movement caught the corner of his eye.

Turning in the saddle, he looked across the range to where a trio of riders topped a rim and swung their horses in the direction of the circling turkey-vultures.

Taking out his off-side Colt, Danny thumbed three shots into the air. Instantly the trio brought their mounts to a halt, looking in his direction. Sweeping off his hat, Danny waved it over his head and the three men put their spurs to the horses, galloping toward him. Three shots fired into the air had long been accepted as a signal for help, one which would only rarely be overlooked or ignored. The three men might be as interested, as Danny had been, in the circling vultures, but his signal took priority over the sight.

Danny studied the men as they approached. Two of them were cowhands; a leathery man of middle-age, plainly dressed and with a low-hanging Dance Brothers revolver at his side; the second looked around Danny's age, a freckle-faced, red-haired young man, cheery, wearing a flashy bandana and red shirt and belting an Army Colt in a cheap imitation of a contoured, fast-draw holster. From the two cowhands, Danny turned to study the third rider. He sat a good horse with easy grace. Although his clothes looked little different from the other two, there was something about him, an air of authority and command, which said "boss" to range-wise eyes. A Remington Beals Army revolver hung butt forward at his left side and looked like he could use it. Not that the man bore any of the signs of a swaggering, bullying gunslinger, but merely gave the impression of being mighty competent.

"You got trouble, friend?" asked the third member of the trio.

"Not me," Danny answered. "But those two fellers down there—man, have they got trouble?"

"Two?" put in the youngest rider. "Reckon it's Sammy and Pike, Buck?"

"Best way to find out's to go look," replied the third man. "Name's Buck Jerome, friend, this's my range. These gents are my foreman, Ed Lyle and Tommy Fayne, he rides for me."

"Howdy. I'm Danny Forgrave. Best go down there and take a look though."

Accompanying the men down the slope. Danny studied their reactions as they looked at the tragic scene in the clearing. He could read little from the two older men's faces, but guessed the scene hit them hard. On the other hand, Tommy Fayne showed shock, his face paled under the tan and his lips drew into tight lines.

"It's Sammy and Pike!" he said in a strangled voice. "That damned murdering skunk Gooch killed them."

"Easy, boy," Jerome said, laying a hand on Tommy's sleeve. "We don't know for sure it was him who did this."

"Who else but a stinking murdering bounty hunter'd gun down two kids like Sammy and Pike without giving them a chance?" Tommy answered hotly. "They weren't neither of 'em good with a gun, and you know it, Buck."

"Hosses are tied, Buck, that's why they never come back," Lyle said quietly. "Happen this feller hadn't found them, they might have laid here for days."

"Might at that," admitted the rancher and turned to Danny. "No offense, but how did you come to find them? You know how it is when you find something like this, questions have to be asked."

"Sure," Danny agreed. "I was headed for those buzzards when I put up a herd of pronghorns and they went down into this hollow. Only they came bursting out like the devil after a yearling. Got me curious to find out what spooked them. I figured it might be either bear, cougar or wolves and that I might be able to pick up a few dollars on its hide. So I came down and found this."

All the time Danny spoke, he felt the other three's eyes on him taking in every detail of his dress and appearance. Not that he had any need to fear detection on that score. Before leaving Austin, Danny dressed for the part he aimed to play. He retained his hat, boots, gunbelt and saddle, but the rest of his clothing no longer bore the mark of a good tailor. Instead he wore a cheap, gaudy bandana, a blue flannel shirt and faded, washed-out jeans. Not was there anything out of the ordinary in the arrangement. Many young cowhands bought the best they could manage in saddlery, hats and gunbelts, but took what they could afford for the rest of their clothing.

After studying Danny, Jerome and Lyle exchanged glances. Both had reached the same conclusion—and just the one Danny wanted folks to make about him. Although this soft-spoken youngster wore two guns and looked proficient in their use, he had none of the ear-marks of a proddy trigger-fast-and-up-from-Texas kid. A good cowhand, most likely, and probably one with a yen to see new ranges around him.

"If Gooch shot the boys, why'd he leave 'em here?" asked Lyle, voicing one of the problems which had been worrying Danny.

"He knew I wouldn't pay him," Jerome answered.

"Then why'd he bother shooting?" growled the foreman. "Gooch didn't give a damn whether the cow thieves stole us blind as long as he got his bounty."

"He maybe aimed to take the boys back to the Forked C and claim he downed them on Crither's range," guessed Jerome. "Cut for sign, Ed, see what you can learn while we start loading the boys. We'll have to take them into town and report this to Farley Simmonds."

"If he handles this as well as he done the rest of the stealing, we'll sure see some action," sniffed Lyle and went to obey his boss's orders.

None of the men expected the task of loading the bodies to be pleasant and they were not wrong. While Lyle examined the ground, Danny, Jerome and Tommy wrapped the bodies in their slickers and loaded them, stiff with *rigor mortis* across the two horses' saddles. By the time the task was completed, Lyle had made his examination and came to his boss to report.

"Was another one here," he remarked, coming up with the same conclusions that Danny had earlier. "Smallish, not too heavy-built feller I'd say. Took out *pronto* when the shooting started, with somebody after him, both riding fast. Then the small feller come back later, cut free some calves and led the others off."

"That'd be the ones they'd branded he took," Jerome guessed.

"Maybe that other feller led Gooch so far he couldn't find his way back to here," Tommy put in.

"Could be," admitted the rancher. "Only I can't think of anybody round here as fits that description, smallish and light built. Can hardly believe that Sammy and Pike were stealing from me, neither. Why Sammy was fixing to get his-self married to one of Ella Watson's gals real soon."

"Yeah," Tommy said bitterly. "Sammy and Pike were my pards. They'd never steal from anybody, boss. Maybe they was trying to stop the cow thieves."

"Maybe," grunted Jerome. "Where'd they go last night, boy?"

"Into town. Sammy wanted to see his gal and Pike went along for the ride. I was fixing to go with them, only one of my mounts was needing tending."

Danny listened to the conversation without asking any questions or making any comments. Above all else, he must not show too much knowledge of Caspar County affairs. A chance-passing drifter would be unlikely to know much about the situation and showing that he was acquainted with the affairs of the county would cause suspicion. So he kept quiet and listened, which had always been a good way to learn things one wanted to know.

"Let's go into town," the rancher suggested. "You'd best come along with us, Danny, the sheriff'll want to see you."

"Sure," Danny agreed. "I was headed that way when I came on this lot."

"I'd best take the running irons with me, Boss," Lyle remarked.

"Do that Ed," answered Jerome. "Only don't let

on that Sammy and Pike were using them. I know their folks and they were good kids."

The words increased Danny's growing liking for Jerome. Some men would have started ranting about ingrates, or damning the cowhands as stinking, untrustworthy cow thieves and not giving a damn who knew that the youngsters had gone bad. From Jerome, Danny turned his attention to the younger of the hired men. Clearly Tommy was badly shaken by the death of his two friends. But did he possess any guilty knowledge of how they came to die? Maybe the youngster had an idea of the identity of the third cow thief. Or perhaps he was merely thinking that, but for a stroke of luck, it might be him lying by the fire.

Mounting their horses, the men rode out of the clearing, Lyle and Tommy leading the dead cowhands' animals, each toting its stiff bundle. None of them spoke until they came out on to open land. Then the sight of the whirling vultures recalled what brought them together.

"How about those buzzards?" asked Danny.

"They're on our way to Caspar, we'd best check," Jerome answered. "Ed, go scout around and see if you can track down that third jasper. I'll lead Sammy's hoss in for you."

"Yo!" replied the foreman and gave Danny a calculating glance. "I'll look around real good."

Much as he would have liked to accompany Lyle,

Danny restrained himself. He guessed that the fore-man intended to check on his tracks also, making sure that he was what he pretended to be. Not that Danny blamed Lyle. Under similar circumstances he would have done the same; and Lyle could learn lit-tle enough by back-tracking Danny for a few miles.

While riding toward the cottonwood, Danny started to get an uneasy feeling that he could guess what they would find. So he did not feel unduly surprised when, from over two hundred yards dis-tance, he saw a body lying beneath the spreading branches of the cottonwood.

"Another," Jerome breathed. "Who the hell this time?"

A few seconds later Tommy supplied the answer. "It's Bat Gooch. I recognize that hoss of his there."

At thirty yards Jerome halted the party. "Hold the hosses here, Tommy. I don't reckon Farley Sim-monds'll make much of it, but we'll not muss up the sign in case he wants to come out."

Leaving their horses, Danny and Jerome walked toward the bounty hunter's body. Both kept their eyes on the ground, studying the sign and reading much the same conclusions from what they saw.

"Can you read sign, Danny?" asked the rancher.

"My pappy was a hunting man. Taught me to know whether a foot pointed forward or back."

"Huh huh. Way I see it is that the feller Gooch was chasing got swept off his hoss by a branch.

Fell just here and Gooch left his hoss to come over to him. Only the other feller wasn't hurt bad and started to throw lead. How d'you see it?"

"Just about the same," replied Danny.

However, although he did not intend to mention it, Danny saw more; a whole heap more than the rancher's description of what happened. First thing to strike Danny was the fact that Gooch's gun lay in its holster. No man who knew sic 'em about gun fighting would approach a potentially dangerous enemy without taking the elementary precaution of drawing his gun. Certainly a man like Gooch would not fail to take so basic a piece of self-preservation. The second significant fact to Danny's mind being the powder burning and blackening around the two bullet wounds in the body. Whoever shot Gooch had been close, real close. As the shooter appeared to have been lying on the ground, Gooch must have been bending; no, that would have put him too high to catch the burning effect of the other's weapon's muzzle blast. Which meant either the other had been allowed to rise, or that Gooch knelt by his killer's side.

Only Gooch would never have allowed the other to rise, or knelt by the fallen cow thief's side, without holding his gun and being sure he could shoot at the first wrong move. Gooch knew gun-fighting and had more sense than take such chances with any man under such circumstances.

And there, Danny figured, he had touched the answer to Gooch's apparent folly. On approaching the fallen cow thief, Gooch would have not only held his gun but would most likely to have sent a bullet into the other just to make good and sure there was no danger to his bounty hunting hide—unless he saw something to make him figure he would not need such precautions.

Something that told him the shape on the ground be a woman, not a man.

Maybe Captain Murat's information about the identity of the brains behind the Caspar County cow stealing had been correct after all!

Chapter 7

THE LAWMEN OF CASPAR COUNTY

CASPAR CITY LOOKED LITTLE DIFFERENT, NOR HAD any greater right to such a grandiloquent four letters after its name, than a hundred other such towns that existed on the Texas plains for the purpose of supplying the cowhands' needs for fun and the basic necessities of life. It consisted of at most forty wooden, adobe, or a mixture of both, buildings scattered haphazardly along half a mile of wheel-rutted, hoof-churned dirt going by the title of Main Street. However, Caspar bore the supreme mark of solidarity and permanency which so many other towns lacked; a Wells Fargo stage station and telegraph office stood proudly on Main Street between the adobe county sher-

iff's office building and Ella Watson's Cattle
Queen saloon.

To Danny Fog's way of thinking as he studied
the town, those silvery telegraph wires contained a
menace to his well-being in that they could be used
to obtain information about him far more quickly
than by using the mail services.

The coming of Danny's party, each man leading
a horse bearing a stiff, unnatural, yet easily recognizable burden, brought people from the various
business premises along Main Street. Questions
were tossed at Jerome, but for the most he ignored
them, saving his story to be told to Sheriff Farley
Simmonds.

Among others, some half-a-dozen women and
a couple of men emerged from the batwing doors
of the Cattle Queen, attracting Danny's attention.
At least one of the women caught his eye. Even
without being told, he knew that black-haired,
beautiful woman in the center of the group to be
Ella Watson, female saloonkeeper and maybe the
boss of the cow thieves plaguing Caspar County.
No ordinary saloon-girl could afford such a styl-
ish, fancy light blue gown; a garment more suited
in cut and line to a high-class New Orleans bor-
dello than in the saloon of a small Texas town.
The dress did little to hide the fact that its
wearer's five-foot-seven figure would be something to see. Cut low in front, it showed off a

rich, full bosom, clung tightly to a slender waist, then spread out to eye-catchingly curved hips, although concealing the legs from view. Her face, beautiful yet imperious, carried a look of authority which none of the others showed and set her aside as one above the herd.

"That's Ella Watson, runs the Cattle Queen," Tommy confirmed, waving his hand to a small buxom, pretty and scared-faced blonde girl who stared in wide-eyed horror at the scene.

"You look like you could use a drink," Danny replied. "Soon as we've seen the great siezer, we'll go get one."

"I can use it," Tommy stated.

The great siezer, the cowhand's disrespectful name for the county sheriff, was not in his office; having gone along to the Bon Ton Café with his deputy for a meal, according to one of the gathering crowd of onlookers. Throwing a glance at his two hands—he had hired Danny on the way into town—Jerome gave instructions.

"Go get that drink, but keep it to one or two at most. I'll send word if Sheriff Farley wants you."

Leaving Jerome to take care of the bodies. Danny and Tommy fastened their horses to the sheriff's office hitching rail and then walked back toward the sturdy wooden front of the saloon. The little blonde girl came running from among her fellow workers, making for Tommy.

"What's happened, Tommy?" she gasped. "Who—what——"

"Easy, Mousey," Tommy answered gently, taking the girl by the arms. "Sammy and Pike ran into trouble."

Danny studied the girl. Wide-eyed horror showed on her pretty, naïve face. She was a fluffy, shapely, if a mite buxom, little thing, wearing a short green dress, black stockings and high-heeled shoes. Maybe not too smart, she looked like she would be happy, merry and good company under normal conditions—and clearly Tommy regarded her as something extra special.

"They were in last night," the girl said.

"Who with?" growled Tommy.

"Sammy was with Dora, but he left with just Pike," answered the girl, turning curious eyes in Danny's direction.

"Mousey, this's Danny Forgrave," Tommy introduced, taking the hint. "He's come to ride for Bench J. Danny, meet Mousey, she's my gal."

"Howdy, ma'am," Danny greeted.

"Call me 'Mousey'," she told him. "My real name's Mildred, but I like Mousey better."

"Then Mousey it is," Danny replied.

At the same time as he spoke to the girl, Danny became aware that one of the men standing with Ella Watson studied him carefully. The man wore a low-crowned white Stetson shoved back on his head and a scar ran across his skull just over the right ear, the hair growing white along its line and in contrast to the blackness of the rest. Standing around six foot, the man wore a black cutaway jacket, frilly-bosomed shirt under a fancy vest, black string tie and tight-legged white trousers. Instead of a gunbelt, the man had a silk sash around his waist, a pearl-handled Remington 1861 Army revolver thrust into the left side so as to be available to the right hand. Cold, hard eyes in a fairly handsome, swarthy face, took in every detail of Danny's dress, with due emphasis on the way he wore his guns. For a moment the man stared, then whispered something in Ella Watson's ear, bringing her eyes to Danny.

"Let's go get that drink, Danny," Tommy suggested. "Come on, Mousey, gal."

Taking Mousey's arm, Tommy escorted her into the saloon and Danny followed. Inside he studied the place with interest. For a small cow town, the Cattle Queen sure looked mighty elegant. There were tables and chairs around a dance space for use of the customers; chuck-a-luck, faro and black-jack layouts, the usual wheel-of-fortune stood against one wall. A long, fancy bar with a big mirror behind it offered a good selection of drinks and was presided over by a tall, burly man with side-whiskers and bay-rum slicked hair. The bartender nodded to the new arrivals as they came to the bar and laid aside the glass he had been polishing.

"What'll it be?" he asked.

"Beer for me 'n' Mousey," answered Tommy. "How's about you, Danny?"

"Same'll do for me, *amigo*," Danny replied.

"What's all the fuss outside?" the bartender inquired as he poured the three beers with deft hands.

"We just brought in Sammy Howe, Pike Evans and Gooch," Tommy explained.

"Whooee!" ejaculated the bartender. "What happened?"

"How the hell would I know?" snapped Tommy, the tensions of the day putting an edge into his voice.

A dull red flushed into the bartender's cheeks at the words and his hand went under the counter toward his favorite bung-starter; a most handy tool with dealing with cowhands who forgot their menial position in life.

"I thought Gooch maybe——" he began.

"Thinking's bad for a man," Danny put in quietly. "Especially when you're talking to a feller who's just lost two good friends."

Slowly the bartender turned his eyes to Danny's face. Something in the young man's level, gray-eyed stare caused the bartender to remove his hand from the bung-starter. Having a well-developed judgment of human nature, the bartender knew when to sit back and yell "calf rope," so he backed water. While he might get by bullying a youngster like Tommy, the bartender reckoned he had best not try any of his games with that tall, blond newcomer.

Then a feeling of relief came to the bartender as he watched the women stream back into his room. At the rear of the group walked Ella Watson and the fancy-dressed hardcase who found Danny so interesting outside. With backing like that, the bardog allowed he might be able to chill the blond Texan's milk. However, he remembered that his boss did not go for rough stuff in the rooms, especially at so early an hour and when dealing with cold-sober and unoffending men.

"Feller seems tolerable took by you, Danny," Tommy remarked, nodding to the mirror's reflection. "Ain't hardly took his eyes off you since you come near him."

"It's not often they get a feller as handsome as me around," answered Danny, taking up his drink in his right hand. "Who is he?"

"Name of Ed Wren. They do say he's real fast with his gun. He works here as boss dealer."

The name did more than ring a bell for Danny, it started a whole danged set of chimes going. In fact, Danny knew more than a little about the gun-hand called Ed Wren. Among other things, he knew where the man picked up that bullet scar across the side of his head. A couple of years back

Wren had hired out to prevent trail hands taking on to help drive the Rocking H herd to market. Trouble being that the Rocking H's owner was kin to the Hardin, Fog and Blaze clan and so Dusty Fog rode to his kinsman's aid. Dusty had been the first man Wren tried to forcibly dissuade. That white streak across the side of Wren's skull told the attempt had not been successful.*

Not for a moment did Danny believe Wren had forgotten the incident. Which could account for the gunman's interest in him on his arrival. Although taller than his elder brother, Danny's facial resemblance had always been fairly marked. Even now Wren must be trying to decide if this be co-incidence or if Danny was either the man who shot him, or kin of the man. Either way, Danny found he had a further piece of trouble he must watch for.

Although Ella Watson did not come to the bar, but stood talking with Wren and casting interested glances at Danny, the other girls swarmed forward, eager to hear the news. Tommy looked them over, apparently seeking for one particular face and not finding it.

"Where's Dora?" he asked. "I've something to tell her."

"She's upstairs, taking a bath," replied a buxom,

---

* Told in *Trail Boss* by J. T. Edson.

tough-looking brunette. "Was that young Sammy you brought in?"

"Yeah," Tommy replied.

"What happened?" put in another girl excitedly. "Who shot him?"

Before Tommy could answer, the batwing doors swung open and a tall young man swaggered into the room. Danny studied the newcomer in the bar mirror, not liking what he saw even though the other wore a deputy sheriff's badge. Unless the deputy possessed money of his own, he dressed a whole heap too well and fancy for a junior peace officer in a moderate-sized Texas county and not a rich county at that. From hat to boots, the deputy wore the rig of a cow-country dandy. If the truculent assurance on his sullenly handsome face, the cocky air about him, and the low hanging brace of ivory-handled 1860 Army Colts be anything to go on, he reckoned himself to have something extra special in his presence.

Crossing the room, the deputy halted behind the two cowhands and jerked his thumb contemptuously over his shoulder toward the door. A hard expression, or what he fondly imagined to be hard, came to his face as he snapped out an order.

"All right, cownurse. Un—The Sheriff wants you at his office *pronto!*"

Normally Danny would have obeyed a member of the county law and reserved his comments on the other's impolite mode of address until away from the view of the local citizens, so as not to weaken the other's authority and standing in the community; but for once he did not. Aside from his dislike for the manner in which the deputy spoke, Danny had a part to play in Caspar County. He saw a good chance presented for him to establish his character before the woman who might possibly be behind the cow stealing in the county.

"I've not finished my drink yet," he answered without turning.

Hearing the sniggers of the watching girls, the deputy scowled. He longed to have the kind of reputation which inspired fear, if not respect, in the hearts of all who saw him. So, wishing to grandstand before the girls, he made a mistake. Shooting out his left hand, he caught Danny by the arm and dropped his right hand to the butt of the off-side Colt.

While training as a deputy under his father, Danny was taught never to lay hands on or threaten a man and that he must only place his hand on the butt of his gun when the situation warranted drawing and using the weapon. To Danny's way of thinking other law-enforcement officers should respect the same rule. He did not like the slit-eyed manner in which the deputy studied him, and pegged him as being the kind of

hawg-mean show-off who would gun down an unsuspecting man just to be able to claim he had
made a kill.

So Danny did not aim to give the deputy a
chance. Pivoting around, Danny threw the hand
from his sleeve and tossed the remainder of his
drink full into the deputy's face. Caught unawares,
the deputy took a hurried step to the rear, entan-
gled his spurs and sat down hard on the floor. Although partially winded, the laughter of the
watching girls drove the deputy to worse folly.

"Why, you——!" he began and clawed at the
right-side Colt once more.

Instantly Danny drew his off-side gun and threw
down on the deputy, his thumb cocking back the
hammer and forefinger depressing the trigger as
the Colt's seven-and-a-half inch barrel slanted
down into line on the deputy's body. At the same
moment Danny saw Ed Wren move. Give him due,
the gunman had speed. The fancy Remington
licked out of his sash in around three-quarters of a
second—which explained how he came to fail
against Dusty who could cut a good quarter of a
second off that time. However, Wren could handle
a gun faster than Danny and the young Ranger admitted the fact without shame.

"Drop it, cownurse!" Wren ordered.

"Don't see how you can down me without I get
to put lead into the deputy at the same time, *hom-*

bre," Danny answered, making no move to obey the man's order.

Which statement was true enough. Even a head shot could not save the deputy from taking lead; in fact, one would ensure he did get a bullet in him. Danny held his Colt with the hammer drawn back and trigger depressed. No matter where the lead hit, should Wren shoot, the impact would cause Danny's thumb to release the hammer. From then on the gun's mechanical processes would automatically take over, firing the charge in the uppermost chamber of the cylinder and expelling a bullet through the barrel which lined on the deputy's favorite stomach.

Rank fear etched itself on the deputy's face as he remembered that Wren showed considerable interest in becoming a member of the sheriff's staff on his arrival in town. However, Uncle Farley hired only one deputy and could not take on another, even one of Wren's standing. The gunhand now had a remarkably good chance of creating a vacancy in the sheriff's office by shooting the newcomer.

"Just hold everything!" snapped Ella Watson, stepping forward but keeping out of line of fire. "Ed put up your gun right now." Not until Wren obeyed her order did she turn her eyes to Danny and continue, "And you, cowboy, if you know what's good for you. I know Clyde there acted a mite hot-headed and foolish, but he *is* the sheriff's nephew."

From the woman's tone, Danny could not decide if she gave warning that the sheriff bore strong family ties and would strenuously object to his nephew going home with a .44 caliber hole in his stomach; or that she merely figured any relation of the sheriff could not help acting foolishly. However, Danny reckoned he had made his point and could rely on the woman to prevent any further need of his Colt. Wren had already returned his gun to the sash, so Danny lowered the Colt's hammer on to a safety notch between two of the cylinder's cap-nipples and spun the gun into its holster. Instantly the deputy let out a snarl and reached toward his off-side Colt. Ella Watson stepped between Danny and the deputy, standing squarely in front of the young Ranger and glaring down at the deputy.

"Now that's enough, Clyde. You asked for what you got and if you want to take in the cowhand under arrest, I'll send for Dean Soskice to act for him."

Just who the hell Dean Soskice might be Danny did not know; but the name appeared to have a mighty steadying effect on the deputy. With a menacing scowl, the deputy took his hand from his gun and rose to his feet. Once again he jerked his thumb toward the door.

"You're still wanted down at the jail," he said.

"Why sure," Danny replied. "I'll come right now. My drink's gone now, anyways."

"I'll come with you, Danny," grinned Tommy, eyeing his new acquaintance with frank admiration. "The boss said for both of us to go along. See you after we've done, honey."

"I'll be here," Mousey promised.

"After you, deputy," drawled Danny as they reached the door. "I was raised all polite and proper."

Still scowling, but with none of the cocky swagger which marked his entrance, the deputy preceded the others from the saloon. Ella Watson watched them go and returned to the gunhand's side.

"Well?" she asked.

"Naw. It's not him. That kid's not better than fair with a gun and Dusty Fog's a whole heap faster. Still he looks a whole heap like Fog, except that he's some smaller and not so hefty built."

Watching the gunhand reach up and finger the bullet-scar, Ella Watson felt relieved. A man did not soon forget the feller who marked him in such a manner and licked him to the draw—Ella discounted Wren's story that Dusty Fog shot him from behind—and it came as a relief to know the newcomer was not the Rio Hondo gun wizard.

"I hope that fool Simmonds handles things better than his nephew did," she said. "I'd like to know more about that cowhand. If he's safe, he's just what we want, brash, looks like he needs money—and not too good with a gun."

Clyde Bucksteed did not speak to Danny and Tommy as they walked toward the sheriff's office, nor did he follow them as would a deputy taking in a couple of suspects. Instead he walked before them, conscious that most of the folks who saw the procession knew where he should be if bringing the two in and not merely running a message for his uncle. Already the bodies had been taken from the street, but a few folks hung around in the hope of fresh developments, enough to make sure the story of Clyde's failure to control the cowhands be broadcast around the town.

"Who-all's this Dean Soskice?" Danny asked of Tommy.

"A law wrangler. Not a bad jasper though. Talks real fancy and gets us boys out of trouble should we take on too wild and rowdy comes pay day. He sure has old Farley Simmonds buffaloed. Wouldn't be surprised if Dean's not in there right now."

Knowing the cowhands' usual contempt for law wranglers, Danny looked forward to meeting this Dean Soskice who buffaloed the county sheriff. On entering the sheriff's office, Danny found his wish granted. Not only was the sheriff-buffaloing law wrangler present, but Danny also found himself face to face with the remainder of the Caspar County law.

Simmonds proved to be a florid-featured, sullen-looking man, run to fat and with an air of lassitude about him. For all that he dressed well and looked a whole heap more prosperous than he should. Unlike his range-dressed nephew, Simmonds wore town-style clothing and sported a gunbelt from which he must be able to draw the fancy-looking Prescott Navy revolver in no less than three seconds starting with a hand on its butt.

Although not one to judge by first appearances, Danny decided that he did not care for Caspar County's law-enforcement officers. With Simmonds and his nephew running the sheriff's office, Danny could well imagine that the county would be full of cow thieves. In fact, he felt considerably surprised that Caspar County did not serve as a haven for more types of outlaws. From what Danny could see, any help he might require locally would not come from the sheriff's office and he doubted if the secret of his identity would remain a secret for long should he take either Simmonds or the deputy into his confidence.

From Simmonds, Danny turned his attention to the other two occupants of the room. Jerome sat by the sheriff's desk, chewing on the end of a thick black cigar and looking mean as hell. The other

man caught Danny's main attention, being the
lawyer who buffaloed sheriffs.

Even with the type of man Danny figured the
sheriff to be, the young Ranger could hardly believe that he would allow Dean Soskice to bother
him. Soskice proved to be a tall, slim young man
with long, shaggy brown hair, a pallid, slightly
surly face and an air of condescending superiority
about him; dressed in an Eastern-style suit, shirt
and necktie, none of which showed any signs of
lavish attention having been spent on them. As far
as Danny could see, Soskice did not wear a gun
and in Texas at that period seeing an unarmed man
was even rarer than finding one walking the street
without his pants. Nothing about the lawyer told
Danny how he managed to buffalo Sheriff Simmonds and Danny reckoned it might be worthwhile to try to find out the reason.

"You're the young feller as found the bodies,"
Simmonds stated in a ripe, woolly politician's
voice, then he turned his eyes to his nephew. "Say,
Clyde, boy, how come you're all wet?"

"He threw beer over me," Clyde answered sullenly.

"Now why'd he do a thing like that?" asked the
sheriff and swivelled his gaze back to Danny. "You
hear me, boy. Why for'd you do that?"

"Feller caught me arm, pulled me around,"
Danny answered. "Next dang thing I knowed,

there he was with my beer all down his fancy shirt front."

Low mutters left Clyde's lips and Soskice moved forward. "If there's a complaint being sworn out against you, cowboy, I'd advise you to tell the truth," the lawyer said, his voice that of an educated Northerner.

"You got a complaint against the feller, Clyde?" the sheriff inquired. "I only telled you to fetch him down here for a talk."

Anger and resentment smoldered in Clyde's eyes as he studied the lawyer's mocking face. However, Clyde recalled other occasions when he had tangled with Soskice on a legal matter and been sadly beaten in verbal exchanges. Soskice knew every aspect of the law as it pertained to working to the advantage of the one Clyde figured on arresting and used that knowledge to build a sizeable following among the cowhands, most of whom had a hefty antipathy toward the peace officers who often interfered with their fun.

"I got no complaint," Clyde finally muttered, knowing Soskice would worm the cowhand out of trouble should he try to make a complaint stick. "The cowhand got me all wrong."

"You'd best tell the sheriff your side of this business, Danny," Jerome remarked. "I've told him the way I saw things and he wants to hear what you've got to say about it."

Just in time Danny prevented himself from delivering the story like a lawman making his report. Instead he told what led up to his discovery of the bodies and left out his own conclusions on the affair.

"Just come on 'em, huh?" grunted Simmonds at last. "Where'd you come from and why'd you come here?"

"Come up from Austin last and happened by this way looking for work."

"Been working in Austin?"

"Nope. Just wanted to see what the big city looked like."

"Where'd you work last?" Clyde asked.

"That's a good question," drawled Simmonds. "Only let me ask 'em, Clyde."

"Sure, Uncle Farley," was the sullen reply.

"Boy's a mite eager, but he's got a good point," the sheriff went on. "Where did you work last?"

"For the Tumbling D, that's Joe Dudley's place down to Ysaleta," Danny answered, giving one of the places Murat named as references.

"And your name's Danny Forgrave?"

"Allus has been," Danny answered.

"It's not a summer name then?" Clyde remarked.

When a man did not wish to give his correct name out West, folks rarely pressed the matter. About the closest one came to doubting the speaker's claim was to inquire whether the title given be a summer name, one taken on the spur of the moment and as a temporary measure.

"Summer and winter both, *hombre!*" Danny growled.

"Danny's working for me," Jerome put in. "You'll find him around the spread if you're not satisfied with his story. Now what're you fixing to do about this cow stealing, Farley?"

"Doing all I can, Buck. Only the county don't pay me well enough to hire more help."

"Then send for the Rangers."

"I wrote a couple of weeks back, but I never heard nothing back," answered the sheriff.

Which, although he did not intend to mention the fact, Danny knew to be a lie. No request for aid sent by a sheriff was ever passed up by the Rangers and his company had received no letter from Simmonds.

"Well, you'd best do something," growled Jerome, "otherwise I'm going to."

"I thought this business today showed you what happened when folk take the law into their own hands," remarked Soskice. "Crither's attempt hasn't been any too successful, has it?"

"I won't be doing it by using a hired killer," Jerome answered, coming to his feet. "Let's go, boys."

After watching Jerome, Danny and Tommy depart, Simmonds gave a grunt. "Buck sounds a mite peeved. He's no fool either and as tough as they come. I sure hope them cow thieves hold off for a spell."

"How about that new cowhand?" asked Soskice.

"His story sounded all right to me," the sheriff replied.

"Why not telegraph Ysaleta and check up on him?" the lawyer suggested. "And don't look so pained, the county will pay."

"Yeah, likely it will," Simmonds admitted. "Clyde, you go down to the telegraph office and send a message to the sheriff at Ysaleta, ask him what he knows about a feller called Danny Forgrave. The answer might make interesting reading."

Chapter 8

MISS WATSON STUDIES DANNY FORGRAVE

~~~

"I DON'T RECKON HE'LL DO A DAMN LOT FOR US," Jerome growled as he left the sheriff's office with Danny and Tommy. "Not unless the cow thieves start branding the stuff out on Main Street."

"Why'd you elect him then?" Danny asked.

"Damned if I know," the rancher admitted. "This's a poor county and there were few enough who wanted to take on the office. Being sheriff's a thankless chore and don't pay more than eating money. Reckon Farley looked about the best of a bad bunch at election time. Let's go grab a meal at the Bon Ton, then take a drink afore we ride out to the spread."

"How about Sammy and Pike?" asked Tommy.

"I'll see about their burying afore we pull out," Jerome promised.

"I mean what're you fixing in to do about them getting burned down that way, boss," growled the youngster. "We ought to see the Forked C bunch and——"

"I'll be seeing Vic Crither," the rancher promised.

"It was through him that they got made wolf bait!"

"Choke off that talk, boy!" Jerome warned. "Vic handled things the way he saw them and he sure as hell didn't tell Gooch to prowl our range."

"He ought to be——!" Tommy began hotly.

"Simmer down, boy," Jerome said quietly. "Vic made a mistake in bringing Gooch in, but he never sent that bounty-hunting skunk on to our range, or told him to gun boys down like that."

"Sammy and Pike were my pards——"

"I know. And they were good boys, too, even if they did go out with running irons by them. But it won't bring them back to start a shooting fuss with the Forked C. All that'll do is get more folks killed. We'll get the same as is happening up in Shelby County and while we're fussing the cow thieves'll steal us blind."

"You're right in that, boss," Danny put in. "I've seen a county that's been torn apart by a range war. The buzzards were the only ones to profit by it."

Jerome looked at Danny with interest. Knowing cowhands, the rancher had not expected support from that quarter. There was something puzzling about the tall blond stranger. Sure he looked and acted like a drifting cowhand, a wild, irresponsible young cuss no different from thousands of others who followed the longhorn trade. Yet he seemed capable of thought; the question about why Simmonds was elected sheriff proved that; and now he talked sense and peace instead of reaching for a gun and panting for war. It said much for Danny's acting ability that he had so far managed his true nature and played a part well enough to fool so shrewd a man as the rancher.

"Just you listen to Danny, Tommy," Jerome grunted. "It's the first time I ever heard a cowhand say anything that made sense—and I've been one. Let's go eat a bite."

While walking toward the Bon Ton Café, leading their horses, the three men saw a bunch of riders entering town. The newcomers came fast, making a fair racket and all showing signs of being in high spirits.

"Rafter O's coming in," Tommy remarked. "Hey, that must be their mean ole bay Joey Jones's leading."

"What's so special about the bay?" Danny asked, studying the riderless horse led by one of the approaching cowhands. It was a fifteen hand, light washy bay animal with a roman nose, little pin ears crimped at the tips and pig eyes, with the general air of a mean one about it.

"Nobody's ever rode it," Tommy explained. "So Rafter O do tell."

"Never yet been a hoss as couldn't be rode," Danny stated.

"And never a cowhand as couldn't be throwed," Jerome countered. "If you're fixing to take that bay on, don't. I saw it one time at Rafter O. It's a suicide bucker and how it's not killed its fool self, or some danged fool rider, I'll never know."

With that the rancher led the way to the Bon Ton where they left the horses at the rail and entered the room to sit at a table by the door. Even as they ordered a meal, a group of the Rafter O men entered and came toward the Jerome table. Danny figured the stocky man in the lead to be boss of the outfit and his guess proved to be correct.

"Howdy, Wally," Jerome greeted.

"Hi, Buck," replied Wally Stirton. "How's things?"

"Could be better."

"They always could. Losing much stock?"

"Lost more than that," Jerome said, knowing the story would come out sooner or later. "Gooch cut down Sammy and Pike last night."

Silence fell on the group of cowhands at the words. While there might be considerable rivalry between the different ranches, most of the hands felt a certain kinship to their fellow workers, especially when one found himself in difficulties. Gooch had never been liked by the free-and-easy cowhands and it might have gone hard for him if he did not already lie dead at the undertaker's shop.

"Where's Gooch at now?" asked one of the Rafter O hands coldly.

"Taking a rest on a slab at Gustavson's," Jerome answered.

"I figured he'd get around to doing it sooner or later," grunted the speaker, for Gustavson was the local undertaker.

"Who got him?" Stirton inquired.

"That's what we don't know," admitted Jerome and told the listening men of his findings on the range.

Knowing cowhands, Jerome figured he had best tell all he knew rather than wait until rumors spread across the range and stirred up bitterness. He did not hide anything, even the fact that his two men had been using running irons when cut down, nor did he excuse Gooch's act on those grounds. Angry mutters rose among the listening men, but all were directed at Gooch and not the bounty hunter's employer.

Danny took advantage of Jerome's speech to study the Rafter O hands. Six in number, they looked like any other bunch of cowhands one might find working on a Texas spread. Three of the six looked to be around Tommy's age and appeared to be badly shaken by what they heard. Danny decided to cultivate the trio in the hope of learning something.

The food came and Danny ate well after a couple of days on his own fixings. When finished, he returned to the Cattle Queen with Jerome and Tommy, after tending to their horses. Already the hitching rail showed a fair crowd inside and on entering the bar room Danny saw that business had picked up. Jerome left the younger men to join a group of prosperous-looking citizens gathered at a side table. For a moment Tommy stood looking around, then led Danny to where Mousey sat with the big buxom brunette.

"Hi, honey," Tommy greeted. "Where-at's Dora?"

"Upstairs," Mousey replied. "She's taking it bad about Sammy."

"She would be," Tommy said sympathetically. "Can I see her?"

Watching the big brunette, Danny thought he saw a smile flicker across her face at the words. Then the expression went as the brunette looked at Tommy and answered. "I don't reckon so. The doctor's been and gave her something to make her sleep. She's took it bad, even if it don't show. Us girls learn to hide our feelings, don't we, Mousey?"

"I know you do, Maisie," the little blonde replied.

"Well, unless one of you boys want to buy a gal a drink, I'll get back to work," the brunette said.

"Call up a waiter, ma'am," Danny drawled. "I'll get them in."

"No beer for me, handsome," Maisie grinned, nodding to a passing waiter. "I like it, but it sure don't like my figure."

"Wine for the ladies," Danny ordered, with the air of a man who wanted folks to assume he had been around. "And fetch a bottle of Stump Blaster for us."

"That's what I like," grinned Maisie. "A big spender."

"Can't think of a better way to get rid of money, Maisie, gal," Danny replied.

As Danny spoke, he saw Ella Watson passing. The saloonkeeper's eyes came to him and studied him in a calculating manner. From the way she looked, Danny figured he interested her and so aimed to keep on with his role of a reckless young cuss who might be open to offers of making easy money over and above his pay.

"When we've had a drink," he went on, "what say we go over and buck the tiger for a whirl."

"Not me," Tommy answered. "Pay day's too far off and I'm saving my money."

"They're fixing in to get married, settle a lil

piece of land and raise kids and cattle, Danny," Maisie explained with a grin, seeing Ella nod toward Danny.

A red flush crept into Mousey's cheeks and she gasped, "How you do go on, Maisie."

"Shucks," Danny grinned. "Marriage's real wonderful. Fact being, I don't reckon any family should be without it."

Maisie laughed with a professional entertainer's heartiness. Having caught her boss's signal and read its meaning correctly, she proceeded to pour out some of the wine brought by the waiter and also to study Danny with careful attention to detail. Before she could reach any conclusions, the Rafter O arrived from the Bon Ton. Halting at the door, the hands looked around the room, their eyes coming to rest on Danny's party. The tallest of the Rafter O group nudged the shortest, nodded in Danny's direction and the whole bunch trouped across the floor, their boss leaving them to join the same group Jerome sat among.

"I tell you, Chuck," the tallest hand announced in a carrying voice, "that ole bay's so mean the boss'll never sell it to Bench J."

"Reckon not, Lanky," the shortest of the party answered. "There wouldn't be nobody at Bench J could ride him."

"I'd bet on that," grinned Lanky.

"How much and what odds?"

All the Rafter O men looked at Danny as he spoke up. Trying to appear as if they had not meant their words to carry to the Bench J's ears, the Rafter O's exchanged glances.

"Did he mean us?" Lanky asked.

"I sure hope he didn't," a red-headed youngster called, with a surprising lack of originality, Red, replied.

"Figure he asked us something," Chuck drawled. "Only does he mean it?"

Coming to his feet and ignoring Tommy's warning glances, Danny dipped a hand into his pocket.

"Do you Rafter O's talk with your money or only your mouths. I said how much do you bet and what odds do you give that I ride the bay?"

"He wants to bet, Chuck," Lanky stated soberly.

"Nope," Danny corrected. "I want to bet money. He'd be no use to me when I won him."

Grins came to the Rafter O faces and cowhands took a liking to Danny. The attempt at getting him to ride the bay was in the nature of a try-out, to see if the newcomer had what it took to make a hand. Whenever Rafter O came into town, their boss specializing in horses more than cattle, they brought along a good bucker in the hope of finding somebody game enough—or fool enough—to ride it.

Everybody's attention came to the table, even the gamblers holding up their games, for the Rafter

O's reputation in such matters was common knowledge and the crowd eagerly awaited developments. If the blond stranger accepted the challenge, and he appeared to have done so, they ought to see some sport.

"Come on, Rafter O," Danny continued after a few seconds. "Make your bet, or set up the drinks."

"We'll give you two to one and take up to sixty dollars," Chuck answered after a brief consultation with his friends. "If you want to go that high."

"Bet!" Danny said loudly and started walking toward the door. "I'll get my saddle. Where'd you want me to ride him, in here?"

"Oh, no you don't!" Ella Watson interrupted, coming forward. "I've an empty corral outside, use that."

Without giving anybody the chance to request that he showed his money, Danny headed for the door and Tommy followed on his heels with Mousey at his side. They went by the front door, but the rest of the crowd headed out at the rear to form up around the big pole corral.

Danny collected his saddle, stripping off the rope, rifle boot and all other extras ready for what he knew would be a hard, gruelling ride. With that done, he took off his gunbelt and handed it to Tommy.

"You watch that hoss, Danny," Tommy warned. "If Rafter O's betting cash money on him, they sure don't aim to lose."

"Nor me," grinned Danny. "Boy, you, me'n' lil Mousey here'll sure have us a time on what we've won."

Together they walked around the side of the building and toward the corral at the rear. Danny watched Chuck lead up the bay, noting that it appeared to be quiet enough and followed without trouble. Not that he felt surprised for a blindfold covered the horse's eyes, and he knew that even a bad outlaw learned the futility of fighting a rope. The bay did not fight having a saddle put on it, but Danny noted the way its ears flattened down and its muscles quivered. That horse as sure as hell did not intend to be ridden by any man.

Like most Texans, Danny had ridden horses almost as long as he could walk. Following his elder brother's lead, Danny took to riding bad ones and became adept at it before he decided the old saying, "A bronc buster's a man with a heavy seat and a light head" had a whole lot of truth and so gave up his ambition of becoming a well-known rider of unmanageable horses. However, a man out West often needed to trim the bed-springs out of a horse or two and Danny had never lost the ability to stay afork a snuffy one. He reckoned he ought to be able to handle the bay unless it proved something really exceptional.

With his health, and wealth, at stake, Danny took no chances. He attended to saddling the horse himself. The spectators noted the care he took in the saddling and nodded their approval.

"No you don't," Danny growled as the horse blew itself out. Bringing up his knee, he rammed it into the animal's ribs and forced a hurried blowing out of the air sucked into the bay's lungs. This reduced the swollen rib-cage to its normal size before the cinches drew tight. If Danny had missed the trick, he would have tightened the cinches on the swollen body and when the bay blew out the air, the saddle was left loose. However, he had seen and countered the move and the saddling went to its completion.

"Are you set to make a start, Danny?" Chuck called, having learned the challenger's name from Maisie.

"Yep," Danny answered and swung into the saddle. Feeling the bay quiver under him, he knew a hard fight lay ahead. "Lord," he thought, "If I get all stove up, Cap'n Jules'll peel the hide off me."

Yet Danny did not ride the horse out of sheer bravado or a desire to grandstand. He wanted to further establish his assumed character in Ella Watson's eyes and knew that if he should be injured riding the horse, Murat would understand his motives.

One thing showed right off. Rafter O might

stand to lose some money but they played fair. Chuck stood at the horse's head and gripped the end of the blindfold, but he made no move to jerk it from the bay's eyes until Danny had settled down firmly in the saddle.

"Now?" he asked as Danny settled in the leather.

"You watch him, Danny," Jerome yelled, giving the friendly, if unhelpful advice always handed out to a man about to start riding a bad one. "He's going to moan with you."

"He'll need to when I'm through, boss," Danny yelled back. "Let her rip, Chuck, boy."

A quick tug removed the blindfold and Chuck went head first through the corral rails in a flying bound which warned Danny, if he needed more warning, of the bay's danger potential. Instantly the horse came apart and without bogging its head down between its legs as did so many of its kind as a starter to bucking. From standing like a statue, the horse took off in a series of crow hops, bounding up and lighting down on stiff legs in an effort to jolt its rider out of the saddle by the force of impact. Crow hopping was not hard to handle for an experienced rider, but Danny knew he could expect much more.

Suddenly the horse reared high, chinning the moon and waving forelegs in the air. However, Danny possessed that rare sixth sense so vital to a bronc peeler in that he could mostly anticipate the horse's moves and be ready to counter them. Up slid his hands along the reins, gripping just below the connection with the bit. He pulled hard, dragging the horse back to its feet before it could crawfish over on to its back and either throw him or crush him beneath it.

Foiled in its attempt, the bay appeared to go wild with rage. It rocketed across the corral, pitching fence-cornered—leaving the ground in one direction, jack-knifing its hind and forefeet together in mid-air and twisting itself to land at about a forty-five degree angle to the place it took off. While the horse went high and landed hard, double shuffling to change its gait with every bound, Danny found little difficulty in riding the leaps.

Then it happened. The bay swapped ends, going up facing north and landing with its head aimed at the South Pole. With his rider's instincts Danny knew he was going to be thrown two jumps ahead of the actual happening. Kicking his feet from the stirrup irons, Danny allowed his body to go limp and landed rolling. He saw the bay bounce away from him and Lanky charged into the corral at a gallop, rope swinging ready to throw. On feeling the touch of the rope, the bay quietened down and allowed itself to be led toward the gate.

"Hold it!" Danny called, getting to his feet. "Bandage him again. I'm not through with him yet."

"What you doing down there then?" asked Chuck.

"Got off to leave him catch his breath," replied Danny and walked toward the bay once more.

On mounting, he started to ride the bay again. Three more times Danny hit the dirt for the bay was one smart horse and knew how to ring in changes of style. It rainbowed high with arched back and shaking head; sunfished in leaping crescents that made it appear to be trying to land first one then the other shoulder on the ground while allowing the sun to burn its belly; fought on a dime, or pioneered new ground with each leaping bounce; straight bucked by going high from all four feet and on the way down tossing its hindquarters up again in the manner of the big paint stallion which crippled Danny's uncle, Ole Devil Hardin.* Through all the tricks, except when sent flying, Danny stayed in the saddle and each time down he rose to mount again. To allow a horse the chance of winding up a winner gave it bad ideas; it happened to the bay often enough to turn the animal into an outlaw.

"Give it up while you're ahead, *amigo,*" Chuck yelled as Danny rose from the fourth throwing.

"Hell yes!" agreed Lanky. "You'll likely get hurt

---

* Told in *The Fastest Gun in Texas* by J. T. Edson.

bad if you don't. He'll go to fighting blind if you keep riding him. We'll call the bets off if you like."

"I *don't* like," Danny replied. "Seeing's how I aim to win your money. Set on that bandage again. He don't know who's boss."

"Now me," grunted Lanky, giving Danny an admiring glance, "I'd say he knows right well who's boss. It's *you* that don't."

"Likely," grinned Danny and headed toward the bay once more.

Standing by the fence, Ella Watson watched Danny mount the bay again. A keen student of human nature, she found Danny interesting and a young man with certain possibilities—if he was what she expected. Her eyes went to Jerome who stood at her side. •

"That's a real game boy," she remarked. "He's new here though, isn't he?"

"Just today rode in," replied the rancher. "It was him found Sammy and Pike. I took him on to ride for Bench J."

Further conversation ended as the bay, given its head, started to buck. A fresh danger had entered the fight, just as Lanky predicted. In addition to the normal risks attendant to riding a bad horse, the bay panicked and began to buck blind; not watching where it went as long as it shook the hated man-thing from its back. Desperately Danny fought to keep the bay's head up; always of prime importance when taking a bad one. However, he had been shaken badly by the throws and felt himself tiring. Night was coming and soon he would not be able to see enough to continue riding. Yet he could see no way of ending the bay's fight.

Twice he just managed to swing the bay clear of the corral rails and prevented a collision. Still bucking blind, the horse charged across the corral, headed for the other side of the enclosure. Only this time Danny felt too exhausted to argue the matter.

"Go ahead, you blasted fool critter!" he growled. "Run in head on and bust your fool neck happen that's how you want it. Only I'm not fixing to go with you."

Yells of warning rang out. Hurriedly those onlookers lining the section of rail toward which the bay rushed leapt backward. Jerome gave a low curse and opened his mouth to yell for the doctor. Everybody watched Danny being carried straight at the rails and expected to see horse and rider pile head-first into the stout timber.

At the last moment Danny swung his right leg forward, up and over the saddle horn, thrusting himself clear. Even as he lit down, he heard the crash of the bay's collision with the corral rails. Only the give of the rails saved the horse from a serious injury and even so the bay rocked backward, staggering and winded by the impact. Danny whirled and ran back, going into the saddle, catching up the reins and applying his spurs. Weakly the bay responded with a few mild pussy-back jumps, arching its back like a hound-scared cat and bouncing up into the air about a third of the height previously managed. Then the horse halted, Danny raked its sides again and brought off another short spell of fighting. The next time Danny used his spurs, the bay stood with heaving flanks and hanging head. Even without the excited and delighted whoops of the crowd who came crowding into the corral, Danny knew he had won. With heaving chest, he slid from the bay's saddle and leaned against the animal's sweat-lathered side.

"Are you all right, Danny?" Tommy asked, reaching the blond Ranger first.

"I—I've—felt better," admitted Danny, then grinned as Lanky thrust through the excited crowd and held out a fistful of money. "Fact being, I feel better right now. Thanks, Lanky. Loser walks the hoss, don't he?"

"Yep," Lanky agreed and shot out a hand to grab a suddenly-departing Chuck by the collar. "Which same you reckoned you'd do it."

"Hell, everybody knows I'm a liar," answered Chuck and reached for the bay's reins. "You wait, I'll get me a ladder, rest it again you, climb up and beat in your knee-caps."

"Go ahead, Chuck," Ella smiled. "I'll save you

an extra big drink. The rest of you, first one's on the house."

Which same started a rush for the saloon. Jerome came over to ask if Danny felt all right and, finding his new hand to be a mite tuckered out but in one piece, slipped a ten-dollar bill into a grimy hand and remarked he had won fifty off the owner of the Rafter O, then joined his party and returned to the bar.

"Go on in, Mousey, Tommy," Ella smiled as everybody else streamed away. "I want to congratulate the winner." After the little blonde and Tommy left, Ella turned to Danny. "You rode well, I never thought you'd get back the last time."

"I had to, ma'am," Danny replied.

"Why?"

"I didn't have any money to pay off with if I lost the bets."

Watching the blond youngster headed for the bar, Ella Watson smiled. Her guess had been correct. A young man that keen to lay hands on money had possibilities and might make a good recruit for her illegal side interests.

Chapter 9

ELLA WATSON HIRES MARTHA CONNELLY

~~~

CALAMITY JANE HATED RIDING ANY KIND OF VEHI-
cle unless she held the ribbons and controlled the
team. So she did not enjoy her trip to Caspar City
and felt relieved when the driver drew rein before
the depot at her destination. Luckily the stage-
coach had not been one of the main runs, or she
might easily have found the driver to be an acquaintance who could let slip her identity and
wind her up in an early grave.

Throwing open the stage's door, the agent gal-
lantly offered his hand to help Calamity alight,
ogling the exposed ankle and lower calf with frank
interest.

"Tuck 'em in, friend," Calamity ordered as she swung herself on to the sidewalk and looked around.

"Huh?" the man grunted.

"Your eyes, they're bugged out a mite. Come down to the Cattle Queen tonight and look all you want, I'll be paid for it then."

Flushing a little, the depot agent jerked around and yelled for the driver to drop down the gal's bags. There were no other passengers to alight at Caspar and Calamity took her two bags, carrying them along the street toward the batwing doors of the Cattle Queen.

"Calam, gal," she mused. "Just keep remembering you're Martha, call me Marty, Connelly. You learned a lot that last night in Austin, don't forget it or you'll be a long time dead."

One thing Calamity had early learned was to face up to the truth. It would do her no good to pretend danger did not lay waiting for her on this chore. To do so might make her careless. So she intended to remember the danger and in doing so would be more likely to recall all the details drummed into her during the evening and morning before she left Austin to start her task.

Sucking in a breath, Calamity pushed open the batwing doors and entered the Cattle Queen's bar room. It was the first time she had ever entered a saloon as a potential employee and she found the feeling novel. The time being shortly after noon, only a few customers sat at the tables or stood by the bar. Looking around, Calamity found only one girl to be present. That one sure looked a tough handful. She had red hair, stood Calamity's size and weighed at least twenty pounds heavier. From the way the red-head's dress fitted her, and the firm muscles apparent in her arms and legs, Calamity figured she would be as strong as they came; the kind of girl Calamity sought to tangle with when employed at her normal trade.

"Looking for somebody?" asked the buxom red-head.

"The boss. That you?"

"Me? Nope. The name's Phyl. I work here. Come on up, I'll take you to the boss. What's your name?"

"Marty Connelly. I'm looking for work."

"Didn't take you for a circuit-riding gal-preacher," Phyl sniffed. "Come on, we'll see Miss Ella."

Following the other woman, and holding down a temptation to plant a kick on the plump butt end so alluringly offered for such treatment, Calamity crossed the room and climbed the stairs. They walked along a passage and Phyl knocked on one of the doors.

"Gal to see you, boss," she said, looking in.

"Show her in, Phyl," replied a female voice.

On entering the room, Calamity took her first look at the woman who might be the leader of Caspar County cow thieves. All in all, Calamity felt a mite disappointed, for Ella had not long been out of bed and wore a dressing-gown which prevented the other girl from gaining any impression of how the saloonkeeper might stack up in a ruckus.

"So you're looking for work," Ella said. "Where were you last?"

"At the Golden Slipper in Austin."

"Why did you quit?"

"That's my business."

Hardly had the words left Calamity's mouth when she felt a hand clamp on her wrist and her arm was twisted behind and up her back in a practiced move. Phyl was strong and real capable; Calamity gave her that as the twisted arm sent a wave of pain shooting through her. Holding down her first instinct, Calamity let out a yelp of pain. She figured showing her considerable knowledge of self-defense might make Ella suspicious and anyway if she tangled with Phyl, win or lose she would not be in any shape to get on with the chore which brought her to Caspar. So, instead of stamping her heel down hard on Phyl's toe then giving the buxom girl an elbow where it would do most good, Calamity stood still and croaked to be released.

"When Miss Ella asks a question," Phyl answered, still holding the trapped arm, "she expects an answer."

Pain almost made Calamity forget her act, but she fought down her desires and whined, "Leggo my arm! I quit 'cause I didn't like it there."

"Why not?" Ella asked.

"T—too much law."

The grip on Calamity's arm relaxed and she brought the limb in front of her to rub the aching wrist. Looking sullen—and promising herself that she would hand-scalp that fat, overstuffed, loud-mouthed, hawg-stupid, cat-house cull before she left Caspar—Calamity awaited the next development.

"Are you in trouble with the law?" Ella inquired.

"Me?" yelped Calamity, trying to sound just right. "Naw! Why should I be?"

"You mean they couldn't prove anything?"

"Yes—no," Calamity answered. "I—I got tired of Austin."

"Then why come here?" Ella asked.

"This's as far as I'd money to go."

While speaking, Calamity watched Ella and gained the impression that the other might be a real tough gal in her own right and not entirely dependent on Phyl to protect her interests.

For her part, Ella studied Calamity with equal

interest. Shorter hair than the usual fashion, a tan to the skin that make-up on the face could not hide, hands roughened by hard work; all the signs of a girl who had spent some time in the female section of the State Penitentiary. A hard cuss, too, or Ella missed her guess. Maybe Phyl had come off easier than she deserved in twisting the newcomer's arm. A telegraph message to the Golden Slipper would clear up the matter of why the girl left Austin. If, as Ella suspected, the town marshal saw the girl on her way for reasons of unproven dishonesty, well, the Cattle Queen had use for such talents.

"What's your name?" Ella said.

"Marty Connelly."

"All right, Marty. I'll take you on. And get this, I run a quiet house. You don't start lifting wallets, or finding a partner to run a badger game—and don't try looking innocent with me—unless I give the word. There's a small place out back, half-a-dozen rooms in it. If you want to sleep with any of the customers, you go there and do it through me and I get all you make. I'll give you your cut out of it. Those are the terms. Take them or leave them."

Wishing she knew more about the working conditions of saloon girls, Calamity did not reply for a moment. She hung her head and stared down at the floor, trying to decide what would be the best answer. Then she made her decision. Ella could not suspect her and be trying to lay a trap. Maybe the conditions might be a mite harsh but probably the saloon keeper figured a girl without money would be forced to accept them.

"All right, Miss Ella," she said. "I'll take on."

"I figured you would," Ella answered mockingly and Calamity knew her guess must be right. "What rooms have we vacant, Phyl?"

"Only Mousey's," Phyl replied. "I'll put her there."

"Huh huh," Ella grunted and nodded her head. It might be as well to keep the new girl in ignorance of the saloon's other business for a time and Mousey knew less than any of the other girls about what went on outside work hours. "See Marty steeled in, Phyl."

"Sure, boss. Come on, Marty."

In the passage, Phyl grinned at Calamity. "You'll find Miss Ella a damned good boss to work for, as long as you play straight by her. If you don't, me 'n' Maisie, she's the other boss gal'll tend your needings and, kid, that's painful."

At that moment the tall, slim, untidy shape of Dean Soskice appeared at the stairhead. The young lawyer slouched along the passage by the two girls, glancing at Calamity in passing and walked toward Ella's room, entering without knocking.

"Who's he?" asked Calamity.

"The boss's lawyer," Phyl grunted. "So you

just keep good and real respectful around him, Marty gal."

"Like that, huh?" grinned Calamity with a knowing wink.

"Just like that. Now me, I'd prefer more muscle on mine."

"And me."

"Well, come on. I'll show you where you bed down. The kid you'll be with's all right and not in your class. There'll be a meal downstairs in about an hour."

Ella Watson looked up from her work as Soskice entered, although she knew that only one person in town would have thought to enter her private quarters without showing the courtesy of knocking first.

"Who was the girl with Phyl?" asked the lawyer.

"A new one. She came in on the stage. Got run out of Austin by the law, and has been in the State Penitentiary or I miss my guess. Anyway, I'll have a message sent to the Golden Slipper asking about her."

"Do you always hire jailbirds, Ella?"

"They're the safest kind. Naïve fools like Mousey are all right for attracting certain kinds of cowhand, but you daren't let her kind know you're doing anything illegal. You can't rely on, or trust, kids like Mousey, but you can trust a dishonest dame as long as she doesn't know too much and has something to lose."

"You should know," sniffed Soskice, sinking into a chair. "Why'd you chance going out with those two cowhands who were killed?"

"They had a small bunch of unbranded stuff but were scared by Gooch. So I went along to show them how safe it was. Only it wasn't. Gooch found us."

"There's nothing to tie you in with them, is there?"

"Not a thing. Don't worry, you're in no danger. Only the two cowhands knew I was going with them. I met them after we closed and wore men's clothing. Nobody would have recognized me, even if they'd seen me. Why didn't you come here before?"

"I—I was busy all yesterday," answered the lawyer.

"What were you doing?" asked Ella bitterly. "Packing ready to run if I was proved to be involved and caught?"

A dull red flush crept into the lawyer's cheeks and sullen anger etched itself on his face. However, he held his comments and thoughts back. Much as he hated to admit the fact, even to himself, he needed Ella Watson's aid to carry out his plans much more than she needed him for hers. Without Ella, he could get nowhere for the cowhands regarded him with amused contempt, ignoring the fact that he bore the results of an Eastern college

education and felt he ought to be honored and re-
spected for it.

"It wasn't that," he said. "You know we have to
be careful. What do you make of the man who
found the bodies?"

"Danny Forgrave? He's a cowhand, likes money
and isn't too worried how he gets it," Ella answered and told about the bets Danny made the
previous evening.

"Sounds a likely one for you then," remarked
the lawyer. "Is he good with his guns?"

"Not better than fair. Either Wren or Stocker
could take him."

"You haven't heard from the packing plant
about the next shipment they'll want, have you?"

"Not yet, but I ought to some time this week.
We've a fair bunch held at the hideout, all wearing
Stocker's brand," she replied then looked in a calculating manner at Soskice. "What're you getting
out of this, Dean?"

"Huh?" grunted the lawyer.

"I'm in it for money. Not because I hate the big
ranchers for working and building something my
old man didn't have the guts, intelligence or ability
to make. I pay the cowhands to steal, to take all
the chances, then get the money back off them in
the saloon. It's all clear profit for me. What do you
get out of it?"

For some reason Ella knew her question would

not be answered. Soskice looked around the room, down at the floor, anywhere but at her and when he spoke, the words had nothing to do with her question.

"The ranchers are getting riled about the stealing. Maybe they'll call in outside help."

"Not another bounty hunter, after what happened to Sammy and Pike," Ella assured him. "And only the county sheriff can call in the Rangers. I don't reckon Farley Simmonds would chance that."

"I don't know about that. He moved fast enough to send to Ysaleta and get word about that cowhand. I saw him on the way here. It seems that Forgrave pulled out of Ysaleta a few steps ahead of being told to go."

"I thought so. That boy'll be useful to us if I can get to him, and *that* won't be hard. But you didn't answer my question, Dean."

"Maybe I do it so I can be close to you."

While Ella doubted if Soskice ever did anything for anybody unless he saw a very good profit motive coming his way, she did not mention the thought. For all his faults, Soskice could sure make love and she reckoned that she might as well get something out of their association.

"All right," she said. "I'll go tell Phyl to send a telegraph message to the Golden Slipper in Austin and find out about Marty Connelly. Go wait in the bedroom and when I'm through we'll see how close we can get."

Not knowing that her *bona fides* were to be checked, Calamity set about making herself comfortable. She took a liking to her roommate from the start and found the feeling mutual. Having only just left her bed—the previous night's celebrations lasted very late—Mousey wore only her nightdress; but she bustled around showing Calamity where to unpack and chattering away like she had not talked for weeks and looked for a chance to do so.

Although the girls' room was anything but grandiose—it consisted of a couple of small beds, a dressing table, washstand and a small cupboard for storing the bulk of their clothes—Mousey appeared to be highly satisfied.

"I never had anything like this before," she told Calamity, clearing her belongings out of two of the dressing-table's drawers. "Always lived in a shack. Six of us kids shared one room, it had a dirt floor and we used to pass down clothes one from the next. Boy, this is living here."

"Yeah," Calamity answered. "Where's a gal take a bath?"

"Down the street at Ling Sing's Chinese Laundry. He runs a bath-house at the back. I'll come with you, but let's grab a meal first."

All in all, Calamity found Mousey to be quite a

talker. By the time they reached the small staff dining room, Calamity knew all about Tommy and the little blonde's intentions in that direction. It seemed that while Mousey enjoyed the glamor of being a saloon-girl, she still appeared to be quite willing to return to a small cabin with a dirt floor—provided Tommy went with her.

"The other girls laugh at me when I talk about it," Mousey said wistfully. "But I know Tommy will marry me as soon as we've saved enough money to buy in on a little place of our own."

On entering the dining room, Calamity began to see the reason for Mousey's almost pathetic eagerness to be friends. All the other half-dozen girls seated around the table appeared to be either older, or at least more suited to the life of a saloon-girl. Brassy, hard-faced, none of them would be the sort of friend an innocent kid like Mousey wanted and most likely her attempts at making friends met with constant rebuffs.

More than any of the others, one girl took Calamity's attention. There was trouble, or Calamity had never seen it. The girl was a blonde, slightly taller and heavier than Calamity, shapely, beautiful; and knowing it she had an air of arrogant truculence about her.

For the rest, they looked like the kind of girls one expected to find in a saloon. Maybe a mite younger and better-looking than one figured on in a small town such as Caspar, but run-of-the-mill. Even the buxom brunette who sat at the head of the table and smoked a cigarette, she would be one of the boss girls and, while looking tough and capable, did not strike Calamity as being out of the ordinary.

"How do you feel, Dora?" Mousey asked sympathetically, going to the blonde.

"Great, how else?"

"But I thought——" the little blonde gasped.

"God! You're dumb!" the bigger girl spat out.

"She's not alone in that," snapped the buxom brunette. "If your brains were gunpowder and went off they wouldn't stir your hair."

An angry glint came into Dora's eyes, but she knew better than give lip to Maisie. So she turned her spleen on somebody else. Her eyes went to Calamity who still stood at the door, taking in the red-head's travel-stained clothing and lack of make-up.

"Who're you?" she asked.

"This's Marty Connelly," Mousey introduced, sounding puzzled. Dora did not act like a girl grieving for a dead lover. If it had been Tommy who—here Mousey stopped herself with a shudder—well, she wouldn't act like Dora did at such a time.

Smarting under Maisie's rebuke, Dora watched Calamity walk toward the table and decided to establish her superiority over the newcomer. Which only went to prove that she had no right to call anybody else dumb.

"Is the boss hiring tramps now?" she sniffed and a couple of her particular friends giggled.

Calamity looked Dora up and down with cold eyes. While she had refrained from handing Phyl her needings upstairs, Calamity figured there must come a time when meekness stopped; and that time had arrived right then. If she allowed Dora to push her around, her subsequent social position would be under the blonde; which Calamity reckoned might be mighty undesirable.

"Looking at you," Calamity said calmly, "I'd say the boss started hiring *old* tramps some time back."

"My my!" Dora purred, twisting around in her chair. "Aren't you cute?"

With that the blonde hurled forward and lashed around her right hand in a savage slap calculated to knock its receiver halfway across the room and reduce her to wailing submission. Only to achieve its object the slap had to land on the other girl first.

Throwing up her left hand, Calamity deflected the slap before it reached her. Before Dora recovered balance or realized just how wrong things were going, Calamity drove a clenched fist into the blonde's belly. The blow took Dora completely unawares, sinking in deep and driving waves of agony through her. Croaking with pain, Dora folded over and caught Calamity's other fist as it whipped up. Dora came erect, a trickle of blood running from her cut lip, and caught a round-house smash from Calamity's right hand. The fist crashed into the blonde's cheek just under her eye and sent her sprawling backward to land with a thud on her butt by the table.

"All right, you alley-cats!" Maisie yelled, throwing back her chair and coming to her feet. "Simmer down. If you want to fight, save it until tonight and do it in the bar for the paying customers."

"I'll take her any time!" Calamity hissed, crouching with crooked fingers as she had seen so many belligerent girls stand at such a moment.

"How about you, Dora?" asked Maisie, knowing the entertainment value of a good hair-yanking brawl between two of the girls.

Dora did not answer, but sat on the floor trying to nurse her swelling, pain-filled eye, soothe her puffing-up lip and hold her aching, nausea-filled stomach, sobbing loudly all the time. Never a popular girl, Dora received little sympathy from her fellow-workers.

Looking down at the blonde, one of the other girls gave a laugh and said, "I don't think Dora feels like tangling with Marty."

Walking to Dora's side, Maisie bent down and pulled the blonde's hand from the eye, looking at the discoloration forming.

"Whooee!" said Maisie with a grin. "That'll be a beauty soon. Anyways, it'll keep you out of the way for a few days. Which's a good thing, the way you're acting. You'd queer the boss's game going on like you are when you're supposed to have lost your own true love. Now shut your yap, or I'll turn Marty loose on you again."

Knowing that Maisie meant every word she said, Dora stifled her sobs. She dragged herself to her feet and limped slowly from the room. Looking around the table, Calamity did not figure she would have trouble with any of the other girls.

Now all she had to do was start learning the proof of the saloonkeeper's part in the Caspar County cow stealing.

Chapter 10

BRING ME HIS WALLET

❦ ～ ❧

ALTHOUGH CALAMITY WONDERED HOW ELLA
Watson would take the news of her actions, no
complaints came down from the boss's office. Over
the meal Calamity became acquainted with the
other girls. She let it be known that she left Austin
at the town marshal's request, but none of the
other girls pressed her too deeply about her past.
Having seen how Calamity handled Dora, a tough
girl in her own right, the rest figured that the red-
head might resent too close questioning and had a
real convincing argument for anybody who tried.
One thing Calamity made sure the others knew,
how Mousey stood with her. Always a generous
and good-hearted girl, Calamity had decided to

take Mousey under her wing and intended to give the friendship the little blonde craved but found missing among the other saloon workers.

After eating, Calamity waited until Mousey dressed and then they left the Cattle Queen. While walking along Main Street toward the Chinese laundry's bath-house, Calamity listened to Mousey's chatter and kept her eyes peeled for some sign of Danny Fog, but saw nothing of him. However, Mousey, telling of the discovery of Gooch and the cowhands' bodies, let Calamity know that Danny had arrived and appeared to be well involved in the business which brought them both to Caspar County.

Even without formal training, Calamity used the best technique for a peace officer involved in such a task; she let the others do most of the talking. With Mousey that proved all too easy. Starved for friendship and loving to talk, she prattled on and gave Calamity some insight into the doings of the area.

"That Dora!" Mousey sniffed indignantly. "She was in love with Sammy, yet she doesn't even look as if she cares about him being killed."

Calamity doubted, from the little she had seen of Dora, if the girl really loved a forty-dollars-a-month cowhand. However, Mousey's words gave Calamity an idea of how Ella Watson ensnared the young cowhands into her cow-stealing organization. Women were far outnumbered by the men out West and the local young cowboys would easily become infatuated by a saloon-girl. After that, the rest would be easy.

"She's a mean cuss all right," Calamity admitted. "Does she pick on you?"

"A little. If I could fight like you do she wouldn't."

"You're danged tooting she wouldn't," grinned Calamity and felt at Mousey's nearest arm. "Say, you're a strong kid. She'd be like a bladder of lard against you if you stayed clear of her and used your fists instead of going to hair-yanking. I'll teach you how, if you like."

Thinking of all the mean tricks Dora had played on her, Mousey gave a delighted nod. "Boy, that'd be great, Marty. Where'd you learn to fight?"

"Here and there. Hey, isn't this the place we want?"

On their return from the bath-house and while waiting for the evening trade to arrive, Calamity began to teach Mousey a few basic tricks of rough-house self-defense in their room. From the way the little blonde learned her lessons, Calamity could almost feel sorry for Dora and next time she tried her bullying.

When Calamity and Mousey reported to the bar room to start work, Dora was nowhere in sight, being confined to her room with an eye that resembled a Blue Point Oyster peeking out of its shell. So Mousey did not find opportunity to put her lessons into practice.

Calamity found the feeling of wearing a saloon-girl's garish and revealing clothing and being in a bar as a worker a novel sensation. Not that she did much work at first. Until shortly after eight o'clock only a few townsmen used the bar and they showed little interest in the girls, having wives at home who took exception to the male members of the family becoming too friendly with female employees of the saloon.

Shortly after eight a few cowhands began to drift in and the place livened. The girls left their tables and mingled with the new arrivals. Laughter rang out, a couple of the games commenced operation and the pianist started playing his instrument. A couple of the customers came to where Calamity and Mousey stood by the bar.

"Hey, Mousey, gal," greeted the taller customer, a cheerful young cowhand sporting an early attempt at a moustache, "Where-at's Tommy?"

"He's not in tonight," Mousey replied.

"Then how's about you and your *amigo* having a drink with me 'n' Brother Eddie?"

"That's what we're here for," Calamity told him. "The name's Marty."

"This's Stan and Eddie," Mousey introduced. "They work for the Box Twelve."

"Sure do," Eddie, a shorter, slightly younger version of Stan, agreed. "Say, what'll you gals have to drink?"

"It'll have to be beer until I've seen Miss Ella," Stan warned.

"My mammy always told me never to look a gift-beer in the froth," replied Calamity.

"Lord, ain't she a pistol?" whooped Eddie. "I'll buy 'em until you get your money off Miss Ella."

A frown creased Stan's face as he glared at his brother. "You hold your voice down, you hear me, boy?"

"I hear you," Eddie answered, dropping his voice. "Hell, these gals are all right, Stan."

"Sure we are," agreed Calamity. "First thing a gal learns working in a saloon is to mind her own business."

Apparently the words mollified Stan for he started to grin again. "Sure, Marty. Only folks might get the wrong idea if they heard Eddie."

"He's only young yet, not like two old mossy-horns like us," Calamity answered. "Say, do we have to stand with our tongues hanging out?"

"Huh?" grunted Stan, then started to grin and turned to the bar. "Four beers Izzy, the ladies're getting thirsty. Say Mousey, where-at's the boss lady?"

"Upstairs, I think," Mousey replied.

"Just have to wait a spell then. Here, Marty, take hold and drink her down."

The beers came and the cowhands drew up their chairs, sitting with Calamity and Mousey at a table. While drinking, Mousey and the cowhands discussed local affairs. Calamity noticed that any attempt to bring up the subject of cow stealing was met with an immediate change of subject by the cowhands. Not that she kept asking questions, but Mousey seemed to be interested as might be expected from one who had been some time in Caspar County. While Stan and Eddy cursed the departed Gooch for a cowardly, murdering skunk, neither appeared eager to discuss why he might have shot down the two Bench J cowhands. Showing surprising tact, Mousey changed the subject and told of Danny's defeat of the Rafter O's bay. A grin played on Calamity's lips as she listened; it appeared that Danny Fog had been making something of a name for himself since his arrival.

"Let's go have a dance," Eddie suggested.

"Sure, let's," Mousey agreed.

Already several couples were whirling around on the open space left for dancing. Calamity, Mousey and the two cowhands joined the fun and it was well that Calamity had always been light on her feet for cowhands did not often make graceful partners. However, Calamity had long been used to keeping her toes clear of her partner's feet when dancing and found little difficulty in avoiding

Stan's boots as they danced in something like time to the music.

Calamity saw the two buxom girls who acted as Ella's lieutenants standing by the bar and watching her. For a moment she wondered if they might be seeing through her disguise. If she had heard their conversation, she would not have worried.

"That Marty doesn't dance too well," Maisie remarked.

There was a considerable rivalry between Phyl and Maisie and the red-head took the comment to be an adverse criticism of her as she took Calamity to see Ella and had her hired.

"Maybe she's out of practice," she answered. "*You* should know they don't go much for dancing classes at the State Penitentiary."

Before Maisie could think up a suitable reply, Phyl walked away. The matter dropped for neither girl felt sufficiently confident in her chances of winning to risk a physical clash that would establish who was boss.

"Hey, Phyl," called Stan, leading Calamity from the dance floor. "Where-at's Miss Ella?"

"She's still up in her room, but she ought to be down soon," Phyl answered. "You wanting to see her real bad?"

"Bad enough. We, me 'n' Eddie's going with the boss to take a herd to Fort Williams and'll be away for a month. I wanted to see if—well, she'll know."

"I'll go up and see her," Phyl promised.

On reaching Ella's door, Phyl knocked and waited.

"Who is it?" Ella's voice called.

"Phyl. It's important."

The door opened and Phyl entered to find Ella standing naked except for a pair of men's levis trousers. This did not surprise the red-head for she knew that her boss had not been in the room all afternoon.

"What's wrong?" Ella asked. "I've only just got back from the hideout."

"It's Stan, that kid from the Box Twelve. He's down there and wanting to see you. Only he's pulling out with a herd and won't be back for a month."

Ella frowned as she went to her bed and removed the pants. Knowing why Stan wished to see her, she did not care for the last piece of Phyl's information. The cowhand had delivered ten stolen yearlings to Ella's men and awaited payment, but she knew that if he rode out with the money her place would never profit by it.

"Who's he with?" she asked, standing clad in her black drawers and reaching for her stockings.

"His kid brother."

"I mean of our girls."

"Mousey——"

"She's no good for what I want," Ella interrupted.

"That new gal, Marty's, with them. Her and Mousey's got real friendly."

"Marty, huh? This might be a chance to find out just what she's like."

"Hey, that reminds me, boss," Phyl put in. "You had an answer to that telegraph to Austin. Marty *was* put on the stage by the town clown, for lifting a drunken dude's wallet."

"I thought as much," Ella stated, drawing on her stockings. "Go down and tell Stan I'll be in soon, and after I've paid him off, you can let me have a word with Marty."

Half an hour later Ella strolled downstairs dressed in her usual work-day style and showing no sign of having sneaked out of town that afternoon, taken a long ride and not long returned from visiting the hiding place of the stolen cattle.

"Did that feller see you-all, Miss Ella?" Stan asked eagerly as she came up.

"Sure, Stan," Ella answered and held out the envelope she carried. "Say, what's in this?"

"Poker winnings, ma'am."

Like the rest of the cowhands who became involved in the cow stealing, Stan believed that Ella merely acted as an innocent go-between for the hard-case Stocker who took the cattle from them. Taking the envelope, Stan opened it and extracted the money. He slipped four of the ten-dollar bills into his wallet and turned to the bar.

"You've been lucky," Ella remarked, watching him thrust the wallet into his hip pocket.

"Sure have, ma'am," Stan agreed with a grin. "This'll sure buy us a time when we get to Fort Williams."

"So you're deserting us, Stan," Ella smiled.

"Shucks, it'll only be for a spell. Say, ma'am, can I buy you a drink?"

"I'll take a brandy, Stan, thank you."

"One brandy, two glasses of whisky, something for the gals and one for you, Izzy," ordered the cowhand. "Say, when's old Pedlar Jacobs coming up here again?"

"Don't know, Stan," replied the bartender. "He comes and goes. What's up?"

"Got him a real fancy white-handled Army Colt last time he was in. I figured I might buy it. Is he a friend of your'n?"

"Not especially," grunted the bartender and moved away to attend to another customer. One thing Izzy did not wish to discuss was his association with Jake Jacobs, particularly before his boss.

"Drink up and have another, gals," Stan told them, ignoring the departing Izzy. "I'm just going out back."

As Eddie elected to go along with his brother, Ella had her chance to talk with Calamity. First Ella sent Mousey off with a message for Phyl, then turned to her latest employee.

"When Stan rides off, I want you to bring me his wallet," the saloon-keeper ordered. "And don't try to look shocked or innocent. I heard from Austin and know why you left town."

"Oh!" said Calamity flatly, not quite sure how she ought to react.

"You don't need to worry about that here, either. As long as you only do it when I tell you. Go to it and lift his leather for me."

"Yes'm," said Calamity.

Yet she felt worried by the assignment even though it presented her with a chance to gain Ella Watson's confidence. Calamity remembered Murat's warning that she must not become a party to any crime by actual participation. Even without the warning Calamity would have shrunk from stealing and did not want the young cowhand believing she was a thief.

At that moment Stan and his brother returned and Ella drifted away. The two young cowhands behaved in a more steady manner than Calamity would have expected, knowing how most of their kind acted when in the money. Although Stan and Eddie bucked down to enjoying themselves, they did not go beyond the ten dollars the elder brother retained for his payment. Of course, ten dollars could get a couple of cowhands reasonably drunk, even when buying drinks for various friends.

"Ten o'clock, time we was riding, Brother Eddie," Stan remarked after bringing Calamity from the dance floor.

"Sure thing, big brother," grinned Eddie. "See you around Mousey."

"Now me," Stan stated, his arm around Calamity's waist, "I've got more good sense than to pick up with a gal who's got a feller. You-all coming to see me on my way, Marty, gal?"

"I sure wouldn't miss it for the world," replied Calamity.

Arm in arm, she and Stan left the room, with Eddie following on their heels. Outside the youngster left his elder brother on the sidewalk while he went to collect the horses. Slipping his arm around Calamity's waist, Stan looked down at her.

"Do I get a kiss afore I leave?" he asked.

"Not out here. Let's go into the alley."

"We're on our way, Marty, gal."

On reaching the shelter of the alley, Calamity turned to face the young cowhand. Like she figured, he might be trying to sprout a moustache and act all big and grown-up, but Stan lacked practical experience in such matters. In her time Calamity had been made love to by some prominent gentlemen, the kind of fellers who could near on curl a girl's hair just by taking her in their arms. Stan did not come into that class by a good country mile.

After fumbling for a moment, he got to slipping his arms around her and brought his face to her own. Calamity slid her arms between his and around his body then burrowed her face to his, kissing him. And when Calamity set her mind to it, she could kiss better than most gals with far greater advantages in more formal education. One thing was for sure, when Calamity started in to kissing him, Stan could have been jabbed by a sharp-rowelled spur and never noticed the pain.

While kissing, Calamity lowered one hand and slid the wallet from Stan's hip pocket. The very ease with which she removed it made Calamity decide to change her plans. On leaving the saloon she had merely intended to give Stan a slight return for a mildly enjoyable evening and then return to Ella Watson with the story that the cowhand did not give her a chance to lift his leather. Finding how easy the removal was, Calamity changed her original plan.

Just before she could put her plan into operation, Stan pulled his head away from her. Calamity found herself in an embarrassing position, standing with the cowhand's wallet in her right hand. Of course, he could not see the hand, but at any moment he might miss his wallet. So, like any good general, Calamity decided the best defense would be to attack.

"Whooee!" she gasped. "You sure kiss up a storm. When a gal's been kissed by you, she sure knows she's been kissed."

Which same coincided with what Stan had always suspected. "Want another?" he inquired.

"What do you think?"

Once again Calamity kissed the cowhand. His arms gripped her tightly, but she managed to extract the money from the wallet. Still holding Stan's attention, she slid the money into his pocket and retained the wallet.

"Stan! Hey, Stan!" Eddie yelled, riding into sight on the street and leading a second horse. "Let's go."

Releasing Calamity, Stan stepped back. Just in time Calamity slipped her right hand behind her back so he could not see the wallet it held. Stan looked at the girl and grinned.

"Dang it, Marty," he said. "I've got to go now. Say, will you be here when I get back?"

"Sure will," she agreed.

Turning, Stan headed for his horse and went afork in a flying mount. A wild cowhand yell left his lips and he put the pet-makers to his horse's flanks. With a few more whooping yells, the brothers galloped out of town. Calamity watched them go, a grin on her face. Quickly she slipped the wallet into the front of her dress and walked back to the saloon.

"Did you get it?" Ella asked as Calamity walked over to her.

"Sure. Where'd you want me to give it to you?"

"In the office. Come on."

Following the saloonkeeper, and with Maisie and Phyl on her heels, Calamity went into Ella's office; a small room with a desk, a couple of chairs and a safe, and used for general saloon business. Taking out the wallet, Calamity handed it to Ella, wondering what would come next.

"What's this?" Ella snapped as she opened the wallet and stared at its denuded interior. "It's empty!"

"Empty!" said Calamity, Phyl and Maisie; Calamity in well simulated surprise, Phyl in a startled tone, and Maisie with a mocking glance at the red-headed boss girl.

"All right, Marty!" Ella hissed. "Strip off!"

"Huh!" Calamity gasped.

"Come on, you know what the boss means!" Maisie snapped, delighted to have scored on Phyl, for the red-head was the one who took the new girl to see Ella.

"All right, don't get mean!" Calamity yelped. "So search me! How was I to know it was empty? I couldn't look in it with him watching, and I'd be crazy to try lifting the cash then bringing an empty wallet."

"She's got a good point there, boss," Phyl put in.

"Or maybe she's just smart," sniffed Maisie. "Peel off, girlie, or I'll do it the hard way."

Normally such a threat would have been met eagerly by Calamity, but she held down her desire to jump the buxom brunette and hand her a licking. Giving a shrug, Calamity peeled off the dress and stood clad in a combined chemise and drawers outfit, stockings and shoes—and with the Remington Double Derringer, borrowed from Captain Murat, in a garter holster. Calamity had hoped to keep her armament hidden from the other saloongirl's eyes but knew her secret was out. All three women looked at the gun, yet none seemed concerned by it.

"You don't need *that* here," Ella remarked, nodding to the Derringer.

"I wouldn't reckon you'd have any virtue to defend," Maisie went on, giving Calamity's dress a thorough search. "I'll do that."

The last came as Phyl started to examine the rest of Calamity's clothing as it was removed. An angry red flush crept to Phyl's face at the words.

"Don't you trust me?" she hissed and made no attempt to put down the garments she held.

"Check the Derringer's got nothing but bullets in it, Maisie," Ella interrupted. "Phyl, go ahead with the underwear."

While she encouraged the rivalry between her two boss girls, Ella had no intention of allowing them to decide once and for all who had the higher social standing by means of a fight. Knowing that hell had no fury like an annoyed or humiliated woman, Ella preferred to let them simmer than have one embittered by defeat and maybe looking for revenge by talking of the saloon's other business to interested parties.

"Nothing," Ella said after the check. "No hard feelings, Marty, but you know how it is."

"Sure, boss. I'm sorry I didn't do better. Why'd you think he had something in his wallet?"

"Just a hunch. It looks like he either changed places, or let Eddie hold the money when they went out back. Young Stan's smarter than I thought. Go back out front and do some work, Marty."

After Calamity left the office, Maisie scowled at Phyl and asked, "Do you reckon she could have hid the money outside before she came in?"

"And bring in the empty wallet?" scoffed Phyl. "She'd need to be real dumb to even think about it. Anyway, we heard those cowhands ride by just before she came in. Stan must have changed the money while he was outside, like the boss said."

"Sure. I think Marty'll work out right for us," Ella stated. "Let's get out and see if there's anything happening."

"We lost some money," Maisie pointed out.

"*I* lost some," Ella corrected. "Don't worry, we'll get it back later."

Out in the bar room Calamity joined Mousey and found the little girl bubbling with curiosity about the reason for the visit to Ella's office.

"It wasn't much," Calamity answered. "The boss just wanted to know if I'd settled in all right."

"Oh! I thought you might have been in trouble. Did you see Stan and Eddie off?"

"Yep," Calamity smiled. "I reckon I did." Then a thought struck her. "Say, when do I get to meet this Tommy of yours?"

"He'll maybe come in tomorrow," Mousey replied. "Hey, if he brings Danny Forgrave in, maybe you and him can make up a foursome with us. You'll like Danny, he's a real nice boy."

Thinking of the night in the Jones cabin beyond Austin, Calamity smiled. "I reckon I might at that."

She figured Danny would take the opportunity to come to town with Tommy and that ought to give them a chance to get together and discuss what they each had learned so far.

Chapter 11

MISS CANARY INVOLVES MR. FOG

～❧～

DANNY FOG COULD NOT TRUTHFULLY ADMIT TO making any progress in the few days spent on the Caspar County ranges. Even with his findings of the first day, he might have been no more than an ordinary drifting cowboy who stopped off at the Bench J for work, for he knew little more about the cow stealing than when he arrived.

Clearly Ed Lyle regarded Danny as being all right when the foreman returned from tracking the remaining cow thief, then back-trailing Danny to establish that the young man had told the truth about coming from Austin City way. The foreman could find no sign that Danny had come from any other direction and so was prepared to treat him as he would any other hand. As to the other matter, Lyle told Danny that the cow thief's tracks disappeared on to the Rock Pile, a large, barren rocky area on the edge of the county and over which following tracks was impossible.

During the next few days Danny rode the ranges and performed the routine work of a cowhand. His skilled use of the borrowed cutting-horse when working cattle lulled any remaining suspicions the foreman might have held, for a cutting-horse was a specialist animal and the fact that Danny possessed one tended to make his pose as a drifting cowhand more acceptable. Mostly Danny worked with Tommy and from the youngster learned much about the affairs of the county. Tommy told Danny how, soon after the stealing became noticeable, Turk Stocker had the other ranchers search his spread on the Rock Pile but they found only his runty, poorly-fed stock on it. So they concluded that the cow thieves ran their stolen animals on to the Rock Pile to make tracking impossible, then could go in any direction to wherever they sold their loot. While Tommy admitted he did not care for Soskice, he said the lawyer had his uses when the sheriff picked up one of the boys. Simmonds appeared to be regarded as a harmless nuisance hired by the town to keep cowhand horse-play in bounds. Of Sammy and Pike's behavior before their deaths, Tommy said little. It appeared that

Sammy found his "love" for Dora came real expensive, far more so than a cowhand could afford and that Pike, like the good friend he was, did what he could to further his *amigo's* romance. Only small things came out of Danny's talks with Tommy, yet they helped him build up a better picture of the situation in Caspar County.

When the story of how Danny stood up to the deputy and Ed Wren made the rounds, and of how he rode the Rafter O's bay reached the ears of the other hands, he found himself regarded as being quite a feller. The feeling pleased him, for this time he had made the grade without anybody thinking of him as Dusty Fog's kid brother and treating him to secondhand respect on that relationship.

However, when Saturday arrived, little had been done to either prevent the cow stealing or find the folks behind it. No further losses had been discovered and none of the crew went out at night to do the necessary riding needed to locate brand and deliver the stolen animals.

"Are you coming into town tonight, Danny?" Tommy asked as they rode toward the Bench J's main buildings on Saturday afternoon.

"Reckon so. I've some money just itching to be spent. Are you fixing to see your gal tonight?"

"Sure am. Why don't you get one?"

"Me? Way I see it, Tommy, *amigo,* ain't but the

one thing worse'n getting left afoot, and that's tying in with a good woman."

"*Compadre,*" Tommy replied soberly, "you'll never know how wrong you are until you've tried it."

"Tell you then," grinned Danny. "Happen I find a real nice gal. I'll think about trying it."

After a meal in the cookshack, the two young men joined the other hands at washing, shaving and generally preparing for a trip to town. Such an occasion called for one's better clothing and the use of one's go-to-town horse; this latter being selected for its good appearance rather than any ability for working purposes. Once prepared, the hands mounted their horses ready for the ten-mile ride to town.

A fair crowd had already gathered in the Cattle Queen when the Bench J crew arrived. Jerome left his hands to attend to a few pieces of business around town, and some of the crew went to deal with personal affairs, but Danny and Tommy headed for the saloon.

"Hey, Maisie!" Tommy called as he entered and looked around the bar room. "Where-at's my gal?"

"Not down yet," Maisie replied. "Set a spell, she'll be along."

"Go grab a table, Tommy," Danny suggested. "I'll fetch in the drinks."

While waiting for Mousey to make her appearance, Danny and Tommy sat at a table and drank beer. Danny looked around for some sign of Calamity, yet she did not appear to be present. Pointing out various people in the room, Tommy named them for Danny's benefit. At last the youngster nodded to a pair of men sitting at a table between them and the stairs leading to the saloon's private quarters.

"That's Turk Stocker and his foreman, Dutchy Schatz," Tommy remarked. "How the hell they manage to make that spread up on the Rock pile pay, I can't figure."

Danny glanced at the men. Both appeared to be tall, Stocker slim and with a whisker-stubbled face, Schatz heavier built, with close-cropped hair and a scarred face that looked tough and mean. Each man wore a gun in a contoured holster and dressed a little more prosperously than might be expected for the boss and sole hand of a run-down ranch in a most unsuitable area. From the little Danny had seen of the Rock Pile, it would prove mighty useless for profitable cattle-raising and be unlikely to provide more than a bare living for its owner. Of course, Stocker could have a side-interest such as hiding wanted outlaws to account for his wealth. Danny decided a visit to the Stocker spread might be worthwhile before his identity as a Ranger became known.

Even as Danny made his decision, he saw Mousey and another girl enter the room. Only when he took a second and longer look did Danny recognize Calamity and he decided his fears that she might have been recognized were groundless. Following the direction of Danny's gaze, Tommy grinned broadly.

"Hey, Mousey's done got company. Look's a right nice gal, too."

"Sure does," Danny agreed.

However, before the girls could arrive at the two cowhands' table, they had to pass where Stocker and Schatz sat. After eyeing the girls up and down, Schatz shot out a hand and caught Mousey by the arm.

"Hi, there, Mousey, gal," he greeted in a harsh, guttural voice. "Sit down and have a drink."

"I've already got one ordered," Mousey replied, trying to pull her hand free.

"What, beer with some fool kid?" growled Schatz. "You can do better than that, little gal."

"You let me go!" Mousey yelped.

Tommy's chair went flying backward as he came to his feet and shot across the room. At the bar Ella caught questioning glances from her two bouncers and Ed Wren but shook her head. Things were a mite slow and Ella knew that nothing livened up a Saturday evening better than a fight, provided it did not get out of hand and she doubted if one between the burly Schatz and young Tommy would go too far.

"Get your cotton-picking hands offen her, Schatz!" Tommy yelled as he rushed forward.

While Tommy did not lack guts, he showed a considerable amount of poor judgment in his method of attack. Schatz thrust himself to his feet, still holding Mousey with his left hand. Even before Tommy could land a blow, the burly man's big fist shot out. Running in added force to a powerful blow and Tommy went down like a pole-axed steer.

"Tommy!" Mousey screeched and landed a kick on Schatz's shin with enough force to make him howl and release her. "Tommy!" she repeated and dropped to her knees at the youngster's side.

"Why you little whore!" Schatz snarled and started to move forward. "I'll——!"

"Get your lousy, buffalo-mange stinking, gut-turning self away from her, lard-guts!" Calamity spat out. Lacking her whip, she reached for the neck of the nearest bottle as a means of defense.

Before Calamity could lay hands on the weapon, Schatz turned and caught her by the arm. "I likes a gal with spunk," he told her.

"You like licking kids, too," a cold voice cut in.

Slowly Schatz turned, pulling Calamity around after him. In that he might have counted himself lucky, for Calamity had just been preparing to drive up her knee into his lower regions hard enough to chill down his milk for a spell. However, she refrained as she saw the speaker and hoped that Danny had learned fighting in the same school as his elder brother; because if he had, mister, that unwashed, square-headed, bristle-haired, no-account hard-case was sure as hell due for a real Texas-size shock.

"My, the cowhands are sure snuffy tonight," said Schatz and shoved Calamity away from him, then launched a blow straight at Danny's head.

Only this time he struck at a different proposition to his previous challenger. Danny might not be much older than Tommy, but bore the advantage of training at the hands of masters of the art of rough-house brawling.

Up came Danny's left hand, but he did not clench his fist. With the open palm he slapped Schatz's driving-out right arm in a snappy motion which deflected it away from him. Instantly Danny ducked under the deflected punch and took a short step forward with his left foot so as to halt slightly behind Schatz's back. At the same time Danny brought up his right arm, across Schatz's body to grip the burly man's shirt at the right shoulder. Pushing hard on to the shoulder with his hand, Danny hooked his right leg behind Schatz's left calf and thrust with it. The moves took Schatz by surprise. He gave a startled yell as his feet left the floor and he went over to land on his back.

Calamity gave a sigh of relief. It appeared that Danny had learned fighting at the same source as did his illustrious elder brother. From the expression on Schatz's face as he came up from the floor, Calamity figured Danny was likely to need all the learning he could lay hands on.

Watching Danny's fists come up, Schatz charged at the blond Ranger with big hands raised to grab. Only he fell into the trap Danny laid for him. Danny did not figure to try using his fists against the bigger man—not until after setting Schatz up for them.

Suddenly and unexpectedly Danny raised his left leg and drove it out to land a stamping kick on the other's kneecap, bringing Schatz's rush to a sudden halt. Even as agony knifed through Schatz and he bent to clutch at the injured knee, Danny threw a right-hand punch. It landed hard and with precision on the side of Schatz's jaw and the big man crashed to the floor again. Spitting out curses and blood, Schatz jerked the Colt from his holster but did not get a chance to use it. Danny leapt forward and stamped down with his left foot. A cowhand's boots carried high heels designed to spoke into the ground and hold firm while roping cattle or horses on foot. Human flesh being less hard, it did not stand up well to the impact of a boot heel smashing down upon it. Schatz let out a screech of pain, lost his hold on the Colt and jerked up into a sitting position. Like a flash, Danny kicked up with his other leg. The boot toe caught Schatz under the jaw, snapping back his head and slamming him down again. This time he did not look like he would be getting up to make more trouble.

"Hold it, Stocker!" a voice boomed.

Hearing the order, and the accompanying click as a gun came to full cock, Stocker froze. He had only half rose and his hand still gripped the butt of his gun, but a glance at the main doors of the saloon told him the futility of going further. Holding his Remington ready for use, Jerome stood just inside the doors and Lyle leaned a shoulder against the door jamb at his boss's side.

"Who cut you in, Jerome?" Stocker growled.

"Danny there rides for me," answered Jerome. "What happened?"

"I'd say that Schatz just got round to picking the wrong feller," Lyle remarked calmly, looking to where Danny stood over the burly hard-case.

Ella Watson knew better than allow such a situation to develop too far. So she thrust herself from the bar and walked across the room, taking care not to come into the line of fire.

"All right, boys," she said. "The fun's over." Her eyes went to Stocker and she went on, "I've told you before about Schatz abusing the boys."

"Looks like he picked on one as didn't take to being abused," Lyle drawled and walked to where Mousey helped Tommy to rise. "You all right, boy?"

"Just about," Tommy answered and felt his jaw. "Where's he at?"

"Sleeping. Got his-self all tuckered out," grinned the foreman.

Seeing that nothing more of interest would come from the situation, the occupants of the room resumed their interrupted pleasures. Jerome watched Ella's bouncers haul Schatz from the room, then he turned to Ella and asked what started the fuss.

"It wasn't Danny here's fault," she replied, "Schatz started to rough-handle Mousey and Tommy, then Danny cut in. That boy's some fighter. Dirty, but good."

"Always reckoned it's better to fight dirty and win, than fair and get all licked, ma'am," Danny put in and turned to Calamity. "Say, how's about taking a drink with me, Red?"

"Right with you and the name's Marty, not Red," she replied.

Watching the two walk away, Ella decided that an efficient young man like Danny Forgrave ought to be a valuable asset to her organization. Of late there had been a considerable amount of independence building at Stocker's end and she guessed that the rancher might be figuring he could run the business without her aid. Wren could take Stocker, but lacked the experience in cattle matters to handle the holding of the stolen stock. Given the right kind of bait, say plenty of money, that blond Texas cowhand might make an ideal replacement should Stocker go too far.

For a time Calamity and Danny celebrated in typical cowhand-saloon-girl style, helped by Mousey and Tommy. They had a few drinks, tried the gambling games with Tommy winning a few dollars, danced and generally enjoyed themselves. Ella watched it all, noting the way "Marty" persuaded Danny to spend more and more on her. The girl had the right idea and it seemed that Danny was struck on her. This showed in the way he blocked any other customer's request that the girl danced or joined him. So Ella watched and waited for a chance to speak with her latest employee away from the crowd.

Ella's chance came when Calamity and Mousey left the room to go out back. On their return, the girls found their boss waiting in the rear passage behind the bar room. Telling Mousey to go on in, Ella kept Calamity with her.

"You're handling that cowhand real well, Marty," she said as Mousey went through the door to the bar room.

"Shucks, that's no problem. He reckons I'm the only gal in the world and wants to prove it."

"Keep him going. I want him broke, but eager to come back for more."

"Sure, boss. Say, he wants to go to the cabin with me for the night."

"Take him up on it and sting him for ten bucks. If you can get any more than that off him, it's yours."

"Yes, ma'am," Calamity said eagerly and turned to go.

Shooting out a hand, Ella caught Calamity's arm and stopped her. "Don't act stupid, Marty. No rolling him or anything like that. I want him coming back here all hot and eager for another session. Understand?"

"Yes, ma'am. I understand."

While Mousey did not go to the cabin with the customers herself, she had a fair idea of what went on in it. She wished that Marty would not go, but made no objections when her new friend left with Danny. Sighing, the little girl looked at Tommy and wondered whether she ought to make an exception in his case, then decided against it as they could not afford the money Miss Ella insisted was paid for the loan of a room.

"We're going to have to play this straight, Calam," Danny remarked as he entered the dimly-lit cabin and located the room allocated to them.

"Reckon we are," she agreed with a grin. "I wonder how much can be heard in the other rooms?"

"I don't know, but let's hold our voices down."

Calamity stripped off her dress and sat on the edge of the bed to peel the stockings from her legs. There was not much room in the section allocated to them and the window had heavy drapes covering it. Danny blew out the lamp and blackness descended on the room.

"How's it going, Calam?" he asked, holding his voice down.

"Fair. I don't figure they know me or think I'm anything but what I say I am. And I know how they get the cowhands involved. Fact being, I'm supposed to be involving you right now."

"That figures. Young Sammy was caught like it. He was one of the pair Gooch gunned down."

"I know," Calamity grunted. "Had words with his grieving sweetie, only she wasn't grieving until after I got through with her."

"Know anything more?"

"Not much. Ella's in this real deep, likely behind it. She slips out of the saloon at nights, and sometimes in daylight, dressed in man's clothes and goes off some place."

"Does huh?" said Danny.

His interest sounded plain in his voice and Calamity tried to see him in the blackness of the room. "What's that mean?"

Quickly Danny explained his findings when he located the bodies of the two cowhands, then of the circumstances surrounding Gooch's death. He mentioned the fact that the bounty hunter's gun had been in its holster; and also about the third cow thief, the one who escaped death at Gooch's hands.

"What do you reckon about that?" he asked.

"Same as you," Calamity replied. "Gooch wouldn't've gone up to any man with his gun still in leather, but he might to a woman. I could say she done good for the world if it was her who downed Gooch."

"Maybe," Danny drawled. "Only don't let that stop you finding out all you can. The sooner we nail this business shut the happier I'll feel. Tempers are a mite high about Sammy and Pike. Comes pay day and the Forked C getting to town at the same time as the Bench J, there might be trouble. The boys are sore enough to start it. Say, do you see much of that lawyer?"

"He comes around visiting with the boss. I don't know how he figures in the game though. Reminds me of somebody, only I can't put my finger on it."

"Looks and sounds like one of them radical Republicans who used to run with Carpetbag Davis' bunch," Danny remarked.

"You hit it!" Calamity whooped.

The next instant Danny's hand clamped over her mouth. "Hold it down, hot head!" he growled.

"Sorry, I forgot," she whispered when he moved his hand. "That Soskice acts and talks like that cuss who was strangling the gals early this year in New Orleans. He was one of Henry George's bunch, them Socialists or whatever they call themselves and Soskice carries the same brand."

"Then why's he down here?" Danny mused. "They hate the guts of us Southern folks and I can't see one of 'em coming down here to live unless he'd good reason. We bust up the best reason when we run Carpetbag Davis' bunch of scum out."

"I'll watch him, see what I can learn. Say, how do we play this lot between you and me?"

"Just how Ella Watson wants it. I've been trying to make her think I'm a young hard-case with a yen for money and who isn't too particular how he gets it."

"You've done it," Calamity told him. "I've got to lead you on, get you all broke and eager for more of me. Then she'll move in, or I miss my guess."

"Then that's how we'll play it," drawled Danny.

"What're we going to do right now?" inquired Calamity, sliding into the bed.

For a moment Danny did not reply, then he said, "Well, I *have* paid my ten bucks."

"Danged if I ever afore got paid for *that*," remarked Calamity.

Half an hour passed before either spoke again.

"Say, Calam," came Danny's voice.

"Yeah?"

"How in hell do I mark down that ten dollars on my expenses?"

Chapter 12

I WANT TO STEAL SOME OF YOUR CATTLE

~~~

By Tuesday Danny figured he had set things up to the point where Ella Watson would make him an offer. He spent the night with Calamity on Saturday and took the girl along with Mousey and Tommy on a picnic the following afternoon. Monday evening found him in town again, watched by a worried Mousey as he spent money on Calamity and the redhead urged him to extravagance. All in all, Danny gave a good impersonation of a lovesick young cowhand making a big play for a money-hungry saloon-girl.

Ella Watson walked across the room on Tuesday evening and looked down at Danny as he sat moodily staring into a glass of beer. Knowing the signs, she came to a halt and smiled at him.

"Hi there," she greeted. "You look like a man with worries."

"Reckon I am, ma'am," he replied. "Where-at's Marty?"

"She'll be down soon. How serious are you about her?"

"Mighty serious, ma'am. She's a real nice gal."

"But expensive. A girl like Marty is used to living high on the hog, Danny."

"Yes'm."

"Short of money, are you?" asked Ella sympathetically.

"Not short, ma'am. Flat busted."

"The trouble is that Marty likes money spent on her," the saloonkeeper went on, glancing to where Stocker sat by the door. "That's the way we women are. She loves you, of course, but a girl has to live."

"Reckon so, ma'am. Trouble being, a cowhand's pay don't go far."

"I know. Well, I've work to do. If you want another drink, Danny, tell Izzy to let you have what you feel like and pay me back when you've some money."

"Gee, that's swell of you, ma'am," Danny answered. "I don't know how to thank you."

"Just keep Marty happy is all you need do," she smiled and walked away.

Although Ella did not go near Stocker, Danny saw her nod to the man and then walk into her office. A few seconds later Stocker rose and slouched out of the main doors. For half an hour nothing more happened. Danny crossed to the bar and gave the bartender Ella's message, then asked for another bottle of beer. He took his seat again, sipping the beer and idly smoking.

The batwing doors opened and Danny saw Stocker and Soskice enter. Crossing the room, they halted at his table.

"Mind if we join you?" Soskice asked.

"Feel free," Danny replied, glancing first at the lawyer then looking hard in Stocker's direction. "But I thought——"

"Hell, I had to stand by Dutchy," Stocker interrupted. "He rides for me and comes cheap. Mind, I admit he's a mean cuss when he's likkered."

"Sure!" Danny grunted.

"Liked the way you handled him, though. Have a drink to show there's no hard feelings."

"Couldn't buy you one back," Danny warned.

"Don't expect it. I know having a gal keeps a young feller short of cash."

"It sure as hell does," agreed Danny, wondering why the lawyer sat in on the deal and waiting to find out.

Both men bought Danny a couple of drinks without bringing up anything more than casual conversation. So Danny decided to put out a couple of feelers and see if he could stir anything up.

"You fellers being so friendly and neighborly, it sure riles me that I got to wait to pay day afore I can repay you."

"Reckon you'd like to earn a mite more, afore then?" Stocker asked.

"I sure as hell would."

"Look, boy," the rancher said, dropping his voice. "I got crowded up on the Rock Pile because the big ranchers took all the good land. A fair number of my cattle stray down there. I'd pay well for any you found and brought back."

"How'd I know which was yours?" asked Danny.

"If they'd got the Bradded S brand on 'em, they'd be mine."

"Shucks, I've not seen any Bradded S stuff on our range," Danny groaned.

"How about unbranded stuff?" the rancher inquired.

"You mean unbranded Bench J stock?"

"Under the law, Danny," Soskice put in, "an unbranded animal is property of the man who lays his brand on it."

"Is that the legal law?" asked Danny, wide-eyed and eager.

"It sure is," agreed the rancher. "Hell, I bet all the ranchers have branded dozens of mine. You'll only be helping me get my own back. It'd be justice and I'd pay you five dollars a head."

"I'll just bet you would," Danny drawled, a crafty glint coming into his eyes. "I risk a rope for five dollars a head, when you'll likely sell them for thirty. Mister, I may be——"

"Hold your voice down!" Soskice hissed. "You want money——"

"Not bad enough to risk a hemp bandana for that price."

"You risked it when you rode the Rafter O's bay," Soskice pointed out, silencing Stocker's angry growls with a wave of his hand.

"Sure, but for a damned sight more than you're offering," Danny answered. "I'll sell at ten dollars a head, no less."

"Ten doll——!" began Stocker.

"All grown beef. Got me twenty head located right now, not a brand on 'em and ready for picking."

Suspicion glinted in Stocker's eyes. "How the hell——"

"Shucks," drawled Danny. "Word's got around about the cow stealing up here. Why'd you reckon I come. I figured sooner or later I'd tie in with the right folks. Where'd you want 'em bringing?"

Stocker and Soskice looked at each other, then a grin creased the rancher's face. "You're a smart cuss," he told Danny. "Brand 'em someplace and deliver 'em to Bowie Rock. Do you know it?"

"That one with a top shaped like the clipped point of a bowie knife, down by where the Talbot River flows off the Rock Pile?" asked Danny.

"That's the one. I'll be there from midnight until three in the morning tomorrow night. You deliver the cattle and collect your money in town."

"Can't say I like that idea."

"It's the way we do it," Stocker growled.

"And it's better that way, Danny," the lawyer put in. "Safer too. If anybody sees you, you claim you found the cattle straying. They can search you and Turk and not find any money on you, so they can't prove you aimed to sell them to him. And if your boss catches you coming in late and wants to know where you've been, he'll not find you with more cash in your pockets than you should have."

"You fellers look like you've got it all worked out," Danny said admiringly.

"We sure have," agreed the rancher. "Do you want in?"

"Deal me in," drawled Danny, glancing to where Mousey and Calamity entered. I'll see you all tomorrow night."

"What do you think?" Soskice asked as Danny rose and walked to meet the two girls.

"He's a slicker young cuss than I reckoned," answered the rancher.

"Too slick, maybe," said the lawyer. "Of course,

the ones who think they're the smartest always fall for a girl. Watch him, Turk, and if he makes a wrong move, kill him."

"Dutchy'd like the chance to do that," the rancher replied.

Danny managed to get Calamity alone long enough to tell her of his progress, then he left the saloon, collected his *sabino* and rode back to the ranch. On his arrival, he put up the horse and walked across to the main house.

"Like to see you, boss," he said when Jerome answered his knock on the front door. "Can you take a walk down to the corral with me?"

One look at Danny's face told the rancher that something serious was afoot. So, without asking any questions, Jerome stepped out of his house and walked toward the corral at Danny's side. Jerome did not know what to expect. It could be that the youngster had found some serious disease among the stock and wanted his boss to hear of it in privacy. There might be any of a dozen other reasons for the request. Never would Jerome have guessed the real reason for Danny's visit; and when he heard, he could hardly believe his ears.

"I want to steal some of your cattle," Danny remarked casually.

While noted for his skill as a poker player, Jerome could not help coming to a halt and staring at Danny.

"Reckon you'd best take that again—slow, Danny."

Reaching into the concealed pocket built into his gunbelt, Danny extracted his badge and held it so Jerome could see the star in the circle. "I'm a Ranger in Captain Murat's company and was sent up here to bust up the cow stealing."

"Well, I swan!" swore the rancher. "You sure as hell had me fooled."

"And a few other folks—I hope," drawled Danny and went on to tell the rancher of his activities, including the offer he received. "I want proof enough to take the whole danged bunch into court, boss."

"Then we'll jump 'em when they take the cattle," Jerome suggested.

"It wouldn't do any good. They'll just claim they know nothing and it's two men's word against mine. I figure to learn where they hide the stock, who they sell to and bring in the whole danged bunch."

"We'll play it your way. Say, can I let Ed in on this?"

"Sure," Danny confirmed. "I'll need help to handle the stuff, too."

"Don't reckon me or Ed'd do for that," grinned the rancher.

"Or me. Can't see them being dumb enough to buy a rancher or his *segundo* becoming cow thieves. I'll take young Tommy."

"Tommy?"

"Sure. He's got a good head and he's steady enough where Mousey's not involved. If you've still got those two running irons we found by Sammy and Pike, I could use them, too."

"I'll see to it," Jerome promised. "And anything else you may need."

The rancher proved to be as good as his word. Next morning Danny, Tommy and Lyle rode out on what appeared to be an ordinary routine ranch chore, except that the two younger members of the party each carried a running iron hidden under his saddle-skirts.

During the ride Tommy listened with awe and admiration as Danny told what he knew about the cow stealing. Although Tommy had a cowhand's disrespect for local law enforcement officers, he regarded the Texas Rangers as being something real special and his admiration for Danny grew rather than lessened on learning the other belonged to that famous body of men. Eagerly Tommy agreed to help Danny and listened carefully to his instructions.

Being older, Lyle hid his feelings and merely re-marked that he had figured all along that there was more to Danny than met the eye. With his knowl-edge of the range, Lyle took the others to where groups of cattle grazed. Scanning the animals, Danny's party picked out and cut any unbranded grown beef they saw, hazing it ahead of them until they drove twenty head before their horses.

"We'd best play this the right way," Danny remarked. "Let's use that hollow where the boys were killed to do the branding."

"Sure," the foreman agreed. "I sure as hell never figured I'd be using a running iron on the boss's cattle."

"Or me," Danny admitted. "Say, Ed, I've been kicking a fool notion around in my head. Let's make sure we can identify our stock by running a small Bench J where it won't show, say under the animal's belly."

"You've got a right smart notion," the foreman grunted.

Once down in the hollow where two men died, the three cowhands set to work and branded the stock. While Tommy held the cattle, Danny cut out each animal in turn and led it to where Lyle kept a fire burning and the running irons heated to a glowing cherry-red. Showing his riding and roping skill, Danny put the captured animal down. Lyle hawg-tied it and then burned a prominent Bradded S on the animal's left hip and traced a smaller Bench J under the belly where it would escape notice unless specifically searched for. In range terms, a brand was "something that won't wash off," so the cattle carried a mark of legal ownership as well as the cow thieves insignia.

The hidden brand, known as a "sleeper" became a standard weapon in the war against cow thieves in Texas and more than one light-fingered, wide-looped gent met his just deserts through Danny Fog's "fool notion."

Hard work and skilled handling saw all twenty head branded before darkness fell. With the preparations made, Danny and Tommy left Lyle to carry out the next part of their business; meeting Stocker and selling their "stolen" cattle.

"Good luck," the foreman said as they parted.

"We'll likely need it," Danny answered with a grin.

Turning his horse, Lyle headed back in the direction of the ranch to report to his boss that all had worked out satisfactorily so far. Danny and Tommy moved the cattle a couple of miles from the hollow which held such painful associations for the animals, then halted to wait out the time until midnight.

"Do we take 'em tonight?" asked Tommy as they mounted their horses ready to make for the rendezvous.

"Nope. Not unless we have to. I want them all, from top to bottom, not just Stocker and his bunch."

"All?"

"There's more than just Stocker involved," Danny told him. "All we do is ride up, deliver the stuff and pull out. Then I'm going to trail Stocker to where he hides it. Once we know that, we can move."

"You're the boss," grunted Tommy.

Shortly after midnight the two young men drove their twenty head of cattle toward the rock shaped like the clipped point of a bowie knife.

"Just act natural, Tommy, boy," Danny warned in a low voice.

"I'm as nervous as a hound-scared cat," the youngster groaned back.

"That's how you should be," Danny replied with a grin. "This's the first time you've ever done any cow stealing. Can't expect you to act easy on it. Just follow my lead though—and don't spook."

As they drew closer to Bowie Rock, the two young men saw a pair of shapes ride into view from a clump of scrub oaks at one side of the outcrop. Coming closer, the shapes turned into a recognizable Stocker and his bulky foreman, Schatz. The burly man's right arm looked unnaturally white but Danny realized this to be caused by a bandage around the place where his heel stamped into flesh.

"Hold it!" Stocker growled suspiciously. "There's two of you."

"Needed two to handle the branding," Danny replied. "Anyways, there's two of you, too."

"Who's the other one?"

"Tommy Fayne."

Hearing Danny's reply, Schatz growled something inaudible but Stocker spoke to cover the sound.

"Allus figured you for a 'saint,' Tommy."

"Reckoned I'd never get enough money saved to marry Mousey by sticking to cowhand's pay," Tommy replied.

Relief hit Danny as he heard Tommy's response. While the youngster's voice sounded a mite strained and odd, it held nothing to make the other men suspicious. If they noticed the difference, they would put it down to his nervousness at becoming a cow thief. More than that, the youngster had given the one reason which might turn a loyal cowhand into a cow thief; Stocker had seen at least two other hands go the same way.

Everything appeared to be going the right way, Danny decided—then Schatz, still smarting under his defeat at Danny's hands, damned nigh blew the whole thing into the air. A nasty snigger left the big hard-case at Tommy's words.

"So you're fixing to marry that——" Schatz began.

"Call him off, Turk!" Danny interrupted before the other could finish his insulting words. "If he doesn't stop, I'll muzzle him. And you watch the cattle, Tommy, we don't want to lose 'em now."

The low-spoken warning prevented Tommy

spoiling the business at hand. Like Danny knew, the youngster tended to get a mite hot-headed where Mousey was concerned. Normally Danny would have regarded the loyalty to a feller's gal as being praiseworthy and expect one to defend his sweetheart's honor; but he did not want Tommy tangling with Schatz until after they had finished their business.

Stocker also appeared to desire peace. Being a businessman, if one engaged in an illegal business, Stocker had an eye on his profit and loss account. While he would be paying Danny double the price given to the more naïve local hands, Stocker figured the young cowboy would be worth it. Even in the darkness he could form some idea of the quality of the stock Danny brought for sale. The cattle appeared to be two to three-year-old animals, ideal for marketing and most likely Danny Forgrave knew where more of them could be gathered. So Stocker did not want trouble.

"Go get the lantern, Dutchy," he ordered. "And leave Tommy be, we don't want any fuss. No offense meant, Tommy."

"None took, neither," Danny answered for his young friend. "You sounded a mite edgy when we rode up, Turk."

"So'd you be in my place. It don't do to take chances."

"Sure admire to be working with a careful

man," Danny drawled. "We've only brought twenty head this time."

"Mind if I look 'em over?" asked the rancher.

"Feel free," replied Danny.

Clearly Stocker had the cow stealing business well organized. On his return from the clump of trees Schatz carried a bull's-eye lantern and directed its light on the "stolen" stock. While a longhorn was dangerous to a man afoot, one could approach the animal while riding a horse without any great risk. Closing on the twenty head, Stocker examined their running iron brands in the light of the lantern. Watching the two men, Danny felt tension mounting on him but held it in check. His right hand rested on the butt of his off-side Colt, for if Stocker discovered the sleeper brands under the cattle's bellies Danny reckoned he would need a gun in a hell of a hurry. Across at the far side of the small bunch of cattle, Tommy felt sweat trickle down his face. The youngster twisted restlessly in his saddle and looked toward Danny; but his nervousness attracted no attention for Stocker and Schatz had become used to such a reaction from the cowhands they dealt with when handing over the stolen stock.

After checking each animal in turn, Stocker nodded and Schatz closed the front of the lantern. The rancher rode to where Danny sat his *sabino* and nodded in approval.

"They'll do, Danny. We can use more stuff like this, and I'll keep paying you ten dollars a head—only don't mention it to anybody else."

"You figure a fair profit for yourself, Turk," Danny replied.

"Hell, they don't cost you anything. And I've overheads to meet out of my end," the rancher objected.

"Likely. Want Tommy and me to lend you a hand to move them?"

"Nope. You'd best not be out too late, you don't want to get Buck Jerome all suspicious."

Danny had not expected finding the hideout for the stolen stock to be so easy and was not wrong, however, a man always liked to try to smooth his path if he could. So he went on with something he must not forget to ask.

"How'll I let you know when I've some more for sale?"

"Go to the Cattle Queen. If I'm not there, leave word with Miss Ella. Say you've found some of my strays and want to deliver 'em. She'll pass the word to me and I'll meet you here at around midnight the following night."

"Mighty obliging lady, Miss Ella."

"Sure," the rancher agreed, then went on just a shade too quickly. "She don't know a thing about what I'm doing. When you go in ask her for the envelope the man left and she'll give it to you. You'll find the money for this lot in it. Only don't mention any names."

"I won't," Danny promised. "See you, Turk."

Turning, Danny rode to where Tommy sat waiting for him at the rear of the bunch of cattle. Just as he reached the youngster, Danny heard the drumming of hooves. Somebody was riding through the night, coming in their direction at a fair speed. One thing Danny knew for sure. The newcomer would not be bringing news of joy and good cheer for him and his young friend.

"Coming from town," Tommy said in a low voice, showing again how clear-headed he could be.

"Get set for trouble," Danny replied, swinging his horse to face the suddenly alert and suspicious Stocker and Schatz.

"Stacker!" yelled the fast-riding shape as it drew closer. "Danny Forgrave's a Ranger. Get him!"

Chapter 13

HOLD HER UNTIL I GET BACK

❦

Business was slack in the Cattle Queen. Only Wally Stirton, boss of the Rafter O, a few of his hands and a handful of townsmen used the bar room. Calamity Jane and Mousey sat at a table clear of the men, idly talking and waiting for customers to arrive. Phyl crossed the room and came to a halt by the two girls.

"Aren't your fellers coming in tonight?" she asked.

"Don't look like it," Calamity replied. "It's gone nine now and no sign of them. They'd've been in afore this if they was coming."

"Things are always quiet on Wednesdays," Mousey went on.

At that moment the batwing doors opened and a man entered, halting just inside to look around. Yet he did not have the watchful caution of a hardcase gun fighter who might find enemies inside and wanted his eyes to grow accustomed to the bar's lights after coming from the darkness. Glancing at the door, Calamity stiffened slightly; recognizing Jake Jacobs, the pedlar who sold information to peace officers. For a moment Jacobs stood at the door, then he walked forward in the direction of Phyl and the other two girls. Calamity felt Jacobs's eyes studying her with more than normal care. Maybe he recognized her, although she doubted it. As far as she knew, the pedlar left Austin before she arrived, but he might remember her from some other town. Calamity decided she must find out what brought the man to Caspar.

"Where's the boss, Phyl?" Jacobs asked, giving Calamity another long, searching look then turning to the buxom redhead.

"Up to her office. You want to see her about something important?"

"She'll think so."

Phyl studied the man for a long moment. Knowing that Ella was preparing to ride out and visit Stocker, Phyl did not wish to disturb her boss. However, Phyl knew that Jacobs often brought news of importance and so decided to take him upstairs.

"Let's go see her then," Phyl said. "Only she'll for sure blister your hide if it's not important."

Watching Phyl and Jacobs make for the stairs, Calamity decided she must try to learn what brought the pedlar to town. A couple of the cowhands drifted over and asked Calamity and Mousey to join them. Rising, Calamity told Mousey to go ahead and she would sit in once she had been upstairs to collect a handkerchief.

By the time Calamity reached the head of the stairs she found that Phyl and the pedlar were just entering Ella's room. Calamity waited until the door closed, then walked over and halted by it. Glancing along the passage, she could see no sign of life. However, she wished she knew where Maisie might be as the big brunette had not been in the bar room. Calamity did not wish to be caught eavesdropping at Ella's door, especially by Maisie for the brunette disliked her due to her friendship with Phyl. Seeing no sign of Maisie or any of the other girls, Calamity placed her ear close to the door and listened to the muffled, but audible conversation inside. She only heard a few words before deciding it had been a good idea to come up and take a chance to discover Jacobs's business.

In the room Ella Watson sat behind the table and looked at Jacobs with cold, speculative eyes. For his part, Jacobs stared back with frank interest. On his arrival, Ella had been about to change into the clothes she wore when riding the range on visits to the stolen stock's hiding place. At such a time Ella wore men's clothing with only a pair of drawers beneath the shirt, levis, boots and jacket out of sight and pulled on her robe. While this covered her naked torso, it gave more than a hint of her state of undress underneath.

"This's private, Miss Ella," Jacobs said, glancing at Phyl.

"Likely," the saloonkeeper replied. "Spit it out, Jake, and put your eyes back in, it won't do you any good."

"I got something to tell you," the pedlar told her, jerking his eyes away from the valley between her breasts.

"I didn't think you'd just dropped in to pass the time of day."

"Just come up from Austin way," Jacobs went on, not put out by her apparent lack of interest.

"So?" asked Ella calmly, although she did not feel calm inside. The nearest company of Texas Rangers had their base in Austin as she well knew.

"So I heard something as might interest the right folks up here."

"I'm busy and tired, Jake. Come to the point, or let's miss you?"

"I'm a poor man, Miss Ella," the pedlar whined. "Not like these cow thieves up this ways."

"Let's have it!" Ella spat out, opening the table drawer and taking out a five-dollar bill. "Damned if I know why I'm bothering, but if you've something interesting you can have the five."

"I hear tell Cap'n Murat's sent a feller up here to bust the cow thieves."

"Why should that interest me?" Ella asked, trying to keep her voice normal although her throat felt dry and her body cold.

"No reason—'Cepting that if this feller does it, you'll lose a fair few good customers."

"Hey——!" Phyl began.

"I see," Ella interrupted.

Only with an effort could she hold her voice even and Phyl's obvious agitation drew a warning scowl from Ella. Annoyance at the red-head's reactions stiffened Ella and enabled her to hide her true feelings. Clearly the pedlar knew something. In some way he must have learned that she ran the cow-stealing organization. Yet he could not know, unless—at that moment Ella remembered a remark passed a few days before, about her bartender's friendship with Jacobs. Izzy must have sold her out, either accidentally or deliberately. Well, that matter could wait until later. More important right now was to discover the identity of the man sent by Captain Murat. Ella did not underestimate the Texas Rangers. The trouble with a Ranger was that he wore no uniform and kept his badge concealed. There had been one new arrival in the area who claimed to have come from down Austin way, she recalled.

"All right," she said. "Supposing I give a damn for my customers! Who is this Ranger?"

"Like I said, ma'am——" Jacobs started to say.

"I know," Ella cut in, "you're a poor man. Here's twenty dollars. Who is he, Jake?"

There she had the pedlar, but he did not intend to mention the point. While Jacobs had gathered a vague rumor that a Ranger left town headed for Caspar County, he could not learn which member of Company "G" was assigned to the task. However, Jacobs could put two and two together so as to come up with a reasonable answer.

"One of them fellers brought in Choya's bunch of *Comancheros* a few days back. Only he's not in town any more, left near on as soon as he come in. I figure he's the one."

"And his name?" asked Ella.

"Danny Fog. He's Dusty Fog's kid brother."

This time Ella could not hold down her startled gasp. Danny Fog—Danny Forgrave—it must be true. Ed Wren claimed that Forgrave reminded him of the Rio Hondo gun wizard. So he would if he was Dusty Fog's younger brother.

"What does he look like?" she snapped.

"Tall, blond, youngish, not bad looking. Rode a big *sabino* stallion last time I saw him."

"Forgrave!" Ella and Phyl said at the same moment.

Even as they spoke the door of the room flew open.

Calamity had just figured that she must find some way of warning Danny of his danger when she found she had troubles of her own. So interested in the conversation had she been, that she forgot to stay alert. Maisie stepped from her room, took in the sight and crept stealthily along the passage toward the listening Calamity. Instead of hearing the gentle pad of bare feet, Calamity missed the sound. The first knowledge she had of Maisie's presence being when one hand gripped the scruff of her neck and another jerked her arm up behind her back.

Dropping the hand from Calamity's neck, Maisie twisted on Ella's door handle and pushed open the door. Before Calamity could make a move to prevent it, she was shoved into the room.

"What's all this, Maisie?" Ella asked.

"I just caught her listening at the door, boss."

Pain in her trapped arm, and a natural aversion to being pushed around, caused Calamity to take action. Lifting her foot, she stamped the heel down hard on Maisie's foot. The big brunette let out a screech of pain and released Calamity's arm, then started to hop on her other leg, clutching at the injured toes. Before Calamity could turn and take the matter further, Phyl leapt forward and pushed her against the wall. Even as Calamity tensed to throw herself into the attack, Ella rose, jerking open the table's drawer and bringing out the Remington Double Derringer which took Gooch's life.

"Now just hold it right there!" the saloonkeeper ordered. "Phyl, take her gun. Keep back, Maisie."

The latter warning came as the brunette prepared to hurl herself at Calamity and take reprisals for the vicious stamp on her foot. Knowing her boss's temper, Maisie halted and watched, scowling and muttering to herself, as Calamity stood still and allowed Phyl to pull up her skirt and remove the Derringer from its garter holster.

"She's a liar, boss!" Calamity yelped, getting her defense in before the attack began. "I'd only just come up here."

"She was listening, boss!" Maisie screeched.

"All right! Shut it, both of you!" Ella spat out. Her fingers drummed on the table top, then she frowned as she remembered that Calamity came to town from Austin. "How many Rangers did Murat send, Jake?"

"One. That Danny Fog like I told you," the man replied, staring at Calamity once more. "Say, I seen that gal afore somewheres."

"In the Golden Slipper at Austin, you skinny goat!" Calamity snapped. "You come up here to tell the boss how I got throwed out of town. I knew you'd got me marked down from the minute you come into the bar downstairs."

"Hell, you saw the way he looked at me right from when he come in, Phyl," Calamity said, turning to the red-head.

"He sure did, boss," Phyl agreed and glared at Maisie as the girl gave a disbelieving sniff.

"How about it, Jake?" Ella inquired.

"Sure I looked at her. Thought I'd seen her around someplace. Only I don't reckon it was in Austin."

"Where'd it be?" asked Maisie, going back to rubbing her aching foot.

"Sure it was Austin, you danged fool!" howled Calamity. "You come here to tell the boss that I'd been run out of town. I've heard about you."

"What've you heard, Marty?" purred Ella, watching the Jewish pedlar's face rather than studying Calamity's expression.

"That he'd sell his own mother if he thought the price was right," Calamity replied. "Hell, I saw him talking to Cap'n Murat down a back street in Austin a couple of days before——"

"That's a damned lie!" Jacobs screeched, and no other word could describe the sound.

"Just stay right where you are, Jake!" Ella ordered, swinging the Derringer in the pedlar's direction.

"Hell, Miss Ella," whined the pedlar nervously.

"Murat only stopped me to ask about a gun I'd tried to get for him."

The pedlar did not make his words sound very convincing and Ella's suspicions deepened. If "Marty" told the truth, Jacobs would just have reached Austin after his visit to Caspar City. So he might have been selling information which brought Danny Fog to Caspar.

"All right, Jake," Ella said. "I believe you. You'd better get going and let me talk with Marty here."

Turning, Jacobs hurried from the room. His one desire was to collect his wagon and put as many miles as possible between himself and Caspar City, for Ella's words had not fooled him at all.

"You letting him go, boss?" Maisie asked after Jacobs left.

"Go get Wren," replied Ella, which answered the question after a fashion. When Maisie left the room, Ella turned her eyes to Calamity. "I'm not sure about you, Marty. Hold her until I get back, Phyl."

"Sure, boss," Phyl replied. "Come on, Marty, we'll wait in my room."

"Wait," Ella ordered, rising and removing her robe. "You saw a lot of Danny Forgrave, Marty. Do you think he might be a Ranger?"

Calamity's first instinct was to scoff at the idea, then she decided not to appear certain. She figured

Danny could take care of himself, and had her own escape to think about.

"Seemed a mite slicker than most cowhands," she admitted. "Only I thought he was just more crooked than most."

Which just about coincided with Ella's judgment of Danny's character. The saloonkeeper drew on the man's shirt, taken from its hiding place and slipped into a pair of levis pants. Watching Ella, Calamity remembered what Danny told her about Gooch's death. Calamity studied the bare flesh under the shirt as Ella fastened its buttons and formed her own conclusions.

A knock sounded on the door as Ella finished buttoning the levis. She called "Come in!" looking at Phyl and Calamity as Wren entered followed by Maisie. "Take Marty to your room, Phyl," Ella went on.

"I'll go with her," Maisie growled.

Anger etched a scowl on Phyl's face, but she did not argue. Phyl and Maisie escorted Calamity to their room, leaving Ella to give orders to the cold-eyed hired killer.

Although she hid the fact, Calamity felt worried. Danny Fog's life hung in the balance and somehow she must try to escape then warn him that his secret had been sold out. Yet before she could do anything, Calamity must escape from the two buxom, powerful boss-girls. For once in her life

Calamity knew fighting was not the answer. She might be able to take one or the other girl, but not both at once; and even against one of them, skilled bar room brawlers that they were, she would be in no condition to make a hard ride straight after the fight.

The boss-girls shared a room slightly bigger, but not much better equipped than the type used by the ordinary female workers. On entering, Maisie leaned her back against the door and stood scowling at Calamity. None of them spoke for almost ten minutes. Calamity sat on the edge of Phyl's bed and the redheaded boss-girl crossed the room to look out of the window.

"Girlie," Maisie finally said, "I sure as hell hope you don't come up with the right answers."

"Why?" asked Calamity. "So it'll put Phyl in bad with the boss."

Turning from the window, after seeing Wren and Ella leave by the side door, Phyl scowled across the room at Maisie. Suspicion glowed in the red-head's eyes and she said:

"You may have something there, Marty."

"Sure I have, Phyl," Calamity answered, taking her chance with both hands. "You've seen how she's always trying to put you in the wrong."

"I don't reckon I'm going to wait until the boss gets back!" Maisie hissed and thrust herself away from the wall.

Before Maisie could reach Calamity, Phyl blocked her path. "You'll leave her be, fatso. She's——"

Drawing back her arm, Maisie swung it, hand knotted into a fist, against the side of Phyl's cheek. The blow landed hard, sending the buxom redhead staggering. Maisie knew she had started something she must finish with Phyl before attempting to handle Calamity. So the brunette hurled herself at Phyl and walked into a punch between the eyes which stopped her in her tracks. The long pent-up hatred burst like a wrecked dam wall and the two buxom women tore into each other with flying fists, grabbing fingers, kicking feet, oblivious of everything except for their dislike of the other and desire to injure her as badly as possible.

While Calamity would have liked to stay through the fight and enjoy what looked like being a hell of a brawl, she knew time would not permit her to do so. Letting the two women become fully engrossed in their hair-yanking brawl, Calamity headed for the door and left the room. She ran along the passage and into her own quarters, closing its door behind her. Even while running along the passage, Calamity had been stripping off the cheap jewellery. In the room, she jerked off her dress and kicked aside her shoes. Opening the cupboard door, Calamity lifted out the grip in which she brought her spare saloon-girl clothing.

Before Calamity left Austin, a saddler worked all night to fit a false bottom into the grip. Reaching into the apparently empty grip, Calamity pulled up the cover of the false bottom and lifted out her normal clothing. The loss of her Derringer did not worry her, for her gunbelt, Navy Colt and bull whip all lay in the hidden cavity and Calamity had managed to keep the gun clean even while working in the saloon.

Outside Calamity's room voices sounded. She could guess what had happened. Hearing the sounds of the fight between Phyl and Maisie, the other girls were coming up to investigate. Moving fast, Calamity drew on her shirt, then pulled the levis pants on over her stockings. Her kepi and moccasins came next, then she slung on the gunbelt and when she thrust the bull whip into her waistband, she felt at ease for the first time since accepting this chore.

Most of the girls stood in the passage outside Phyl and Maisie's room and from the sounds beyond the door there had been little easing of the fight. One of the chattering, excited girls happened to glance in Calamity's direction, then gave a yell which brought every eye to the transformed redhead. None of the girls made a move, but Dora scowled and opened her mouth.

"The name's Calamity Jane, gals," Calamity announced before Dora could say a word. "I'm working with the Rangers to bust up this cow stealing and I've no fuss with any of you."

Most of the girls had nothing to lose by the wrecking of the cow stealing organization and anyway that bull whip looked a damned sight too dangerous for them to start arguing. However, Dora still hated Calamity for the humiliation handed out on the red-head's arrival. Now she saw a chance to take her revenge.

"Get he——!" she began.

Once more Dora was interrupted. Mousey did not know for sure what was happening, or why her friend Marty dressed in men's clothes and claimed to be Calamity Jane. All the little blonde knew was that she now had a good chance to tangle with Dora and put Calamity's self-defense lessons into use. Catching Dora by the arm, Mousey turned her and brought across a punch which staggered the bigger blonde back across the passage.

"Why you——" Dora hissed.

Down went Mousey's head and she charged, ramming Dora full in the middle of the body. In her childhood, Mousey lived hard and still had strong little muscles. These, backed by the lessons Calamity gave her, enabled her to tangle with Dora and make the bigger girl believe a bobcat had jumped her.

"Sic her, Mousey!" Calamity whooped. "And use your fists like I taught you."

The other girls let Calamity depart unhindered. Unlike Mousey, Dora had never been popular, so the girls saw no reason to halt what shaped up to be a good fight; especially as Mousey appeared to be getting the best of it.

Wally Stirton, boss of the Rafter O, his men and the other customers gathered at the foot of the stairs, listening to the screeches, yells and other sounds of female brawling which drifted down. Then the men stared as Calamity came into sight and ran down the stairs toward them.

"What the hell?" Stirton growled. "Hey Marty——"

"Get your boys on their hosses and lend me a mount, Wally," Calamity interrupted. "We've a chance to bust up the cow stealing."

Give him his due, Stirton threw off his surprise and got moving without wasting time or asking fool questions. He and his men headed for the door on Calamity's heels and the girl told him her true identity, also of Danny's danger.

"Lanky's out back with one of the gals," Stirton drawled as they left the saloon. "Take his dun, Mar—Calamity."

At that moment the sheriff and his deputy came running along the street. Calamity did not give them time to start asking questions, but pointed to the saloon and yelled, "There's a fight upstairs, Sheriff!"

Then she and the Rafter O men hit their saddles. Before the sheriff could ask any of the questions which boiled up inside him, the entire bunch went racing out of town. In the lead Calamity told Stirton to head for Bowie Rock. She rode as never before. Knowing it to be a race against time—with Danny Fog and Tommy Fayne's lives hanging in the balance.

Chapter 14

IT WON'T WORK THIS TIME, ELLA

~ ~

DANNY FOG AND TOMMY FAYNE HAD ONE ADVANtage over Stocker and Schatz when Ella Watson screamed out her warning. The two young men knew they were fakes and both expected trouble as soon as they heard the rapidly approaching horse coming from the direction of town.

Even though Danny could not figure out how Ella discovered his secret, he wasted no time in idle speculation. Already he held a Colt in his right hand for he had never professed to be real fast with a gun and knew he could not match Stocker in a straight draw-and-shoot fracas. Even as the rancher heard the words, let out a startled curse and grabbed for his gun, Danny went into action.

"Yeeah!" Danny yelled and fired a shot into the air.

Never the most stable and easily handled of animals, even less so when newly branded and being held against their will during the night hours, the longhorns needed little encouragement to spook and take to running. All twenty head heard the yell and crash of the shot, then they went to running—straight at Stocker and Schatz. While a longhorn could be handled, under normal conditions, safely enough from the back of a horse, that did not apply right then. Both rancher and segundo took one look at the wild-eyed, charging animals and jumped their horses clear of the rush of scared longhorns.

Cattle streamed by Stocker as he threw two shots at Danny. Shooting from the back of a horse had never been noted as an aid to accuracy, especially when using instinctive alignment, so the bullets missed the Ranger. Danny fired in return—only he took the extra split-second to raise his Colt shoulder high and use the sights, and his *sabino* stood like a statue under him. Flame licked from the barrel of Danny's Colt and the muzzleblast blinded him for an instant. When his vision cleared, Danny saw Stocker pitching down from his saddle. Even as he saw Stocker fall, Danny heard the crackle of shots to his right.

Tommy had drawn his Colt even as Danny

started the cattle running. Often Tommy day-
dreamed about becoming involved in a gun fight
and now he found himself tangled in a real shooting match. Buck-ague sent rippling shivers of excitement through the youngster and his hand
shook at he threw up the Colt. Guns roared and
Tommy heard a flat "splat!" sound which he failed
to recognize as the cry of a close-passing bullet for
he had never heard one before. He saw the bulky
shape of Schatz charging at him and shooting as he
came. Only the fact that Schatz handled his gun
with his left hand saved Tommy from death. Three
times the burly man fired, his lead coming closer
with each successive explosion.

Pure instinct guided Tommy's hand. He lined his
Colt, feeling his horse fiddle-footing nervously
under him and guessing the movement helped to
save his life. Tommy never remembered firing his
Colt. All he knew was that the gun roared and
bucked against his palm. Next moment Schatz
tilted backward, sending a bullet into the air, and
went down from his horse, landing under the feet
of Tommy's mount and letting the gun fall from his
hand.

Tossing his leg over the *sabino's* saddlehorn,
Danny dropped to the ground and moved toward
Stocker. The rancher had come to his knees, but
saw Danny approaching and noted the gun the
Ranger held. Remembering the lawman's rule for

dealing with such a situation, Stocker released his injured right shoulder and raised his left hand hurriedly into the air.

"Don't shoot, Ranger!" he yelled. "I'm done. Hold your fire."

The rancher appeared to be making more noise than one would expect; or so Danny decided. With every instinct alert and working full-time, Danny soon discovered the cause of the noise. Dark shapes moved out of the clump of scrub oaks from which Stocker and Schatz had emerged. Even as Danny saw the shapes, guns bellowed from them and muzzle-blasts flared in the darkness—but not aimed in his direction.

"Hit the ground, Tommy!" Danny yelled, throwing two shots at the shapes and changing his position as he fired.

Showing remarkable presence of mind considering it to be his first involvement in a corpse-and-cartridge affair, Tommy left his saddle and lit down on the ground. Although his horse spooked, it did not go far with the reins trailing but came to a halt a couple of hundred yards away. Crouching behind a black mound, Tommy raised his Colt. Then he realized that the hump hiding him was in reality Schatz's body. The man lay without a move.

"If you shoot, Tommy," Danny called, rolling over as he spoke and sending another shot at the approaching men, "move straight after it."

Before Tommy could profit by Danny's advice, they heard more hooves thudding from the direction of Caspar City. So did their attackers. Coming to a halt, the Stocker men read danger in the approaching riders, for they knew one set of hooves could not make so much noise.

"Get out of here!" yelled a voice.

Not that the speaker needed to give any warning. Even before he yelled out his sage advice, the others had turned and started to run back in the direction from which they came. In his excitement Tommy thumbed off two shots, but failed to make a hit.

Stocker saw his hired help take a Mexican stand-off and painfully dragged himself on to his hands and knees after flattening down to allow his men to shoot without fear of hitting him. Holding his bullet-busted shoulder with his left hand, the rancher prepared to make a dash for safety.

"Hold it right there, Stocker!" Danny barked, coming to his feet and lining the Army Colt. "I won't tell you twice!"

Knowing that nobody would blame a Texas Ranger for shooting down a cow thief, and not being sure whether Danny would carry out the threat or not Stocker came to a halt. Crashes and the snorting grunts of disturbed horses told the rancher that his men were going fast and that he had no hope of escape.

"All right," he said. "I'm done."

"Danny!" yelled a voice from the approaching party. "It's the Rafter O!"

"Come ahead," Danny replied.

Bringing his horse to a halt, Stirton pointed off to where the fleeing Stocker hands could be heard. "Want for us to take after them?"

"Nope. They'll not be back," Danny answered. "How'd you get here just at the right time?"

"That gal Marty told us you was a Ranger and likely to need help. Say, she reckons she's Calamity Jane."

"Don't you going tell nobody now," grinned Danny. "But she is Calamity Jane." He looked around then went on, "Say where is she now?"

"Took off after one of the bunch who cut away across the range. Sent us on in to help you."

"Stay on here and tend to Stocker, Wally. I'll go look for her."

"Is Stocker in on this stealing?" growled the rancher, looking at the suddenly scared, wounded man.

"Up to his dirty li'l neck," replied Danny.

"Then we'll hold him for you," Stirton promised.

Something in the rancher's voice brought Danny to a halt as he started to turn away from Stirton.

"I want him alive when I get back," Danny warned. "You hear me?"

"Danged if you aint' a spoilsport," grunted Stirton. "He'll be alive and kicking when you come back."

Turning, Danny walked to the waiting *sabino* and swung into the saddle. He looked to where a couple of the Rafter O hands stood over Schatz's body, one of them holding the bull's-eye lantern and directing its beam downward. Tommy stood to one side and even in the feeble light Danny could see the pallor of the youngster's usually tanned cheeks.

"He's done," said the hand with the lantern. "Hit straight between his two eyes. Who got him, Tommy?"

"Let's ride, Tommy," Danny put in before the youngster could answer.

Tommy raised no argument. One of the Rafter O hands had collected his horse and he swung into the saddle.

"I'll tend to things here, Ranger," Stirton called. "Need any of my boys?"

"Reckon me and Tommy ought to be enough," Danny replied. "Fix Stocker's wing and put out some guards in case his boys come back to try and pry him free."

For a time Danny and Tommy rode in silence. Danny looked sideways at Tommy and guessed how the youngster must feel.

"It's never easy, killing a man, Tommy," he said.

"It sure ain't," agreed Tommy. "I felt like

fetching up, only I didn't want Rafter O to see me do it."

"There's no shame in it. Only remember this. It was him or you. He sure as hell aimed to kill you and you'd every right to stop him any way you could."

"Yeah," answered Tommy and gave a shuddering sigh. Then he threw off the feeling of nausea. "Say, how do we find Calamity?"

"Just ride on for a spell, then stop and listen some."

Following Danny's plan, they rode on for about half a mile before halting their horses and sitting in silence. Only the ordinary night noises came to their ears and after a few seconds Danny started his *sabino* moving again.

"Which's the shortest way back to town, Tommy?" he asked.

"Over that ways," Tommy answered, pointing to the right.

Swinging their horses in the desired direction, the two young men continued their ride. Ten minutes passed and Danny brought his *sabino* to a halt again. This time he heard something, so did Tommy.

"What the hell?" Tommy asked, listening to the screams, squeals and scuffling noises that came faintly to their ears.

"Reckon ole Calam done caught up with Ella

Watson and just couldn't resist temptation," Danny replied. "Let's go take a look."

When Ella Watson saw the approaching Rafter O hands even though she did not recognize them as such, she knew her reign as boss of the Caspar County cow thieves had come to an end. From the number of shots and the shouted conversation between Danny Forgrave—or Fog, whichever it might be—and Stocker, she figured that the attempt at killing the Ranger had failed. So she decided to pull out, make a fast ride to town, empty her safe and be well clear of Caspar before the posse could return with news of Stocker's capture.

A yell from the posse told Ella she had been seen and one of the riders spun out of the group to give chase. Ella urged her horse to a gallop, yet she doubted if the animal could outrun her pursuer's mount. Hearing the yell Stirton let to warn Danny of his coming, Ella knew she did not have a chance in a race. The Rafter O specialized in breeding good horses, while her own mount had been selected more for its gentle qualities and steadiness rather than speed.

After half a mile of riding Ella swung her mount in the direction of the distant town and safety. Although still ahead of her pursuer, she figured it would not be long before they came together. Yet she did not wish to kill the one following. With

Gooch it had been different. Then she fled before
a wanton murderous bounty hunter and her life
would have been forfeit if she fell into his hands.
So she decided to use her trick merely to draw her
pursuer in close. Then she would take his horse,
leaving him afoot and unable to interfere, ride
relay with it and her mount, make better time to
town and have a longer start on the posse.

Having made her decision, Ella unbuttoned the
shirt and pulled it open to expose her naked
breasts. With bait like that any cowhand would
walk straight into her trap and fall easy prey to her.

Twisting around in her saddle, Ella glanced back
at the other rider. At the distance separating them
she could not distinguish the other, or recognize
him. It was not Danny For—Fog, of that she felt
sure. However, he might prove too smart to fall for
her trick. Probably the rider was one of Stirton's
younger hands trying to make a name for himself.
If so, he ought to be easy to handle.

Ella's horse slid down a gentle slope and as it
reached the open ground at the bottom she reined
it in. Before the pursuer came into view, Ella slid
out of her saddle, dropping to the ground and
lying flat on her back. She tossed the hat aside with
her left hand, allowing her hair to hang over her
face. With the right she took out her Derringer and
held it concealed. From above came the sound of
the other horse, then the noise ended and she knew

the rider had halted. She figured he could not see enough yet, but would come in closer.

For a few seconds nothing happened. Ella lay still, hardly daring to breathe in case she scared the other rider into shooting in panic. A faint scuffling sound came to her ears as the other started to come down the slope. Any second now he ought to come close en——

"It won't work this time, Ella, gal," said a voice.

Shock ripped into Ella at the words, for she saw the failure of her plan. No man addressed her, but the voice sounded mighty like that of the girl she knew as Marty Connelly. Somehow, Ella could not think how, the girl must have escaped from the Cattle Queen, gathered a posse and ridden to Danny's aid. Cold fury gripped Ella and she tensed to roll over with a roaring Derringer in her hand. Even as the thought came to her, Ella heard the low click of a Colt coming to full cock.

"Don't try it, gal!" the voice went on in cold warning tones. "A stingy gun like that Derringer's no good at over fifteen foot and I'm more than that away."

"What'd you want?" Ella asked, debating whether to chance rolling suddenly and throwing a shot at the other girl.

"Throw the gun well clear of you," came the reply.

"Go to hell!"

"In good time, I reckon. Only this's the last time I'll ask you to throw that stingy gun away."

Ella could tell from the tone of Calamity's voice that argument, or trying to roll over and shoot, would do no good. Being a smart girl, Ella knew when to call the game quits. Carefully she lifted her right hand, then tossed the Derringer a fair distance away across the level floor at the foot of the slope. Then she sat up slowly and shoved her hair back before turning to look at her captor. One glance told Ella the other girl spoke truly in the matter of relative gun ranges. From the casually competent manner the red-head held the Navy Colt, she knew how to handle it and could likely have put a bullet into Ella had the saloonkeeper made a wrong move.

Standing up the slope, Calamity watched the Derringer sail away into the darkness. On her arrival at the head of the slope Calamity had left her borrowed horse standing with trailing reins, hung her whip around the saddlehorn and moved in ready to hand Ella a shock.

"Who are you?" Ella asked, coming to her feet.

"The name's Martha Jane Canary——"

"Mar—Calamity Jane?"

"I've been called worse," Calamity admitted. "Let's ride back to Bowie Rock and meet Danny Fog."

"If he's still alive," answered Ella.

"I figure he will be. That boy's real smart."

"How'd you get away from Maisie and Phyl?"

"They got to fussing with each other after you left."

"I should have figured that," Ella sniffed. "Say, you and I can't come to some arrangement, can we?"

"Sure. You just arrange for yourself to get on that hoss and we'll head back to Bowie Rock."

"You've nothing on me," Ella remarked as she walked slowly toward Calamity.

"Maybe. Only I figure somebody'll start to talk once we begin the round-up and haul them down to the pokey."

Knowing some of her confederates, Ella did not doubt Calamity's words. So she decided to try another line of reasoning, one which might appeal to a young woman like Calamity Jane.

"What have I done that's so wrong?" asked Ella. "All I did was buy a few head of cattle from the cowhands——"

"Don't say you didn't know they'd been stolen," Calamity interrupted.

"Had they? They weren't branded——"

Once more Calamity cut in. "Most of them come from branded herds, and you knew it all along."

"All right, so I knew it. I gave the cowhands a

few bucks. Hell, the ranchers would lose more to the weather or stock-killing critters in a year than I took."

"Losing's one thing. Having 'em stolen's another."

"So who got hurt?" asked Ella.

"How about Sammy and Pike from the Bench J?"

"You can't blame me for that!" Ella gasped, for her conscience troubled her more than she cared to admit over the death of the two young cowhands. "I only happened to be along that night. They always used that same place to brand the stuff. Even if I hadn't been along, Gooch'd've found them."

"And how about Gooch?" said Calamity quietly.

"If you *are* Calamity Jane, you've been around long enough to know what Gooch was. He aimed to rape me before he killed me—Hey, how did you know that I killed Gooch?"

"That was easy. Jake Jacobs told Cap'n Murat you was running the cow stealing. Both me and Danny figured you must have killed Gooch. Gooch might have been as bad mean as a man could be, but he'd a damned sight more sense than walk up to a *man* with his gun in leather. So it figured that a woman killed him and you seemed most likely to be the one. When I saw you coming in wearing those men's duds, I knew how you got Gooch in close and stopped him being suspicious."

"And you blame me for killing Gooch?"

"Nope. For turning decent kids into thieves. Get going."

"Nobody made them steal," Ella pointed out as she walked by Calamity.

"Nope. Only your gals got them so they didn't know which way to turn."

Slowly Ella walked up the slope with Calamity following. Suddenly the saloonkeeper appeared to slip. Ella's feet shot behind her, striking Calamity's legs and tangling with them. Letting out a yell, Calamity went over backward and lost her gun as she fell. Even as Calamity rolled down the slope, Ella stopped herself sliding after the red-head and grabbed up the fallen Navy colt. Coming to her feet, Ella lined the gun down at Calamity.

"It looks like we don't need any arrangement now, Marty," Ella said.

"Reckon not?" replied Calamity. "There's no percussion caps on the nipples."

"We'll see about that," Ella answered and squeezed the trigger.

Instead of the crack of exploding powder, a dull click came to Ella's ears as the Colt's hammer fell on a bare cap-nipple. Fury gripped Ella as she thought of how she had been tricked into tossing aside her fully-loaded Derringer—which used rim-fire bullets and did not need separate percussion caps to ignite the powder charge.

Calamity had not made the move intentionally.

While she had stored the Colt with powder and a lead ball in each of the cylinder's chambers, Calamity knew too much about guns to leave percussion caps on the nipples when the weapon was not in regular use. In her rush to get out and try to save Danny, she clean forgot to put the caps in place and did not remember this basic—and vitally necessary—precaution until just before she caught up with Ella. Then it had been too late, so Calamity made a damned good bluff.

Giving a squeal of rage, Ella charged down the slope. She swung up the Colt and launched a blow aimed at Calamity's head. Bringing up her hands, Calamity caught Ella's wrist as it brought the Colt down. Pivoting, Calamity heaved on the trapped arm and her pull, aided by Ella's forward momentum, sent the saloonkeeper staggering by her. Ella lost her hold of the Colt and went sprawling face down on the ground. Rolling over, she spat out a curse and sat up, glaring at the advancing Calamity.

"Give it up," Calamity ordered. "Or do you want to wrassle it out?"

Seeing that she could not escape unless she got by Calamity, Ella prepared to take action. Quickly Ella hooked her left foot behind Calamity's right ankle, rammed her right boot against the redhead's knee, pulled with the left, hoved with the right, and brought Calamity down on her back. Then Ella reared up and flung herself on to Calamity.

From the moment Ella landed, Calamity knew, as she figured on their first meeting, that the saloonkeeper could take care of herself in any girl's kind of tangle.

Calamity's kepi went flying as two hands dug deep into her hair and damned near tore out a pile of red curls by their roots. Pure instinct guided Calamity's response. Even as she screeched in pain, her own hands hooked strong fingers into Ella's black hair and Calamity braced herself, heaving up then rolling Ella from her. Swiftly Calamity twisted on to the top of Ella, trying to bang the black head against the ground. Not that Calamity stayed on top for long. Over and over the two girls rolled and thrashed. Neither showed any kind of skill, or gave a thought to anything more scientific than clawing hair, swinging wild slaps and punches or biting at first.

Nor did the situation improve for almost three minutes. Then, how it happened neither girl could say, they found themselves on their feet. Ella stood behind Calamity, arms locked around the red-head and pinning Calamity's own arms to her sides. Just what advantage Ella aimed to take from the situation is hard to say. She retained her hold and crushed on the red-head, but could do little more. Gasping in fury more than pain, Calamity lashed backward, her heels landing on Ella's shins hard enough to make the other girl yelp and loosen her hold a little. Then, Calamity clasped her hands together, forcing outward against Ella's grip with her elbows and sucking in a deep breath. Suddenly Calamity exhaled and felt the encircling arms relax their grip. Before Ella could tighten again, Calamity twisted slightly and rammed back with her elbow, driving it into the other girl's stomach.

Giving a croaking gasp, Ella lost her hold and stumbled back. Jumping in to attack again, Calamity discovered that the other girl was far from beaten. Ella's left hand shot out, driving the fist full into Calamity's face, then the right whipped across to connect with the other girl's jaw. Staggering, Calamity caught her balance just in time to meet Ella's rush.

For over ten minutes the girls put up a hell of a fight. They used fists, elbows, feet, knees, punching, slapping, kicking, pushing and shoving. Twice they rolled over Calamity's Colt without giving it a glance or thought. However, Calamity slowly gained the upper hand. Her normal working life offered greater advantages in the matter of staying fit and strong than did Ella's career in the saloon.

Gasping in exhaustion, her shirt torn open and minus one sleeve, Calamity landed a punch which sent the sobbing, exhausted Ella sprawling to the ground. Calamity stumbled forward. Through the mists which roared around her, Calamity heard horses approaching. She came to a halt and started to look at the newcomers. That look nearly cost her the fight. Ella had come to her feet, swaying and barely able to stand. Yet she still swung a wild punch that ought to have flattened Calamity; only it missed the red-head by a good two inches. Once more Calamity's instincts came to her aid. Ignoring the two men who rode toward her, she turned and lashed out with all she had. In missing, Ella staggered forward and walked full into the punch Calamity threw. It clocked like two rocks cracking together as they fell down a cliff, Ella shot sideways, landing face down and lying still. Weakly Calamity followed the saloonkeeper up and dropped to her knees by the still shape.

"Ease off, Calam!" Danny yelled, leaping from his horse and running to where Calamity rolled the unconscious Ella over. "She's done!"

"Know something?" Calamity gasped. "I'm not much better myself."

Five minutes later Calamity recovered enough to tell Danny what had happened. Ella sat moaning on the ground to one side and Calamity looked at Danny with a wry grin as he said:

"I'd swear you let her jump you and get your gun just so you could fight."

"Shucks," grinned Calamity. "Can't a gal have any fun at all?"

Chapter 15

CLEAN UP IN CASPAR COUNTY

~~~

AT NINE O'CLOCK ON THURSDAY MORNING, DANNY Fog stood before the desk in the Caspar County Sheriff's office and looked at Simmonds. The young Ranger had not shaved and looked tired after a night without sleep. Once Calamity patched up her own and Ella's injuries, Danny took them back to Bowie Rock. There he found Stocker to be in a most cooperative mood and from the rancher learned all he needed to know to make sure he could smash the cow stealing in Caspar County forever. Once Danny knew everything, he left Stirton's party to bring in the prisoners and rode ahead. In Caspar City he visited the sheriff's office to offer the local law enforcement officers the chance of winding up the affair.

"And that's how it was, Sheriff," Danny said, finishing his explanation of why he came to Caspar County and what he had achieved. "Ella Watson suckered the cowhands into stealing for her. Then she took the money paid to them back out of their pockets in the saloon. Stocker got all eager to help and talked up a storm."

"Where'd he hide the stolen stuff?" asked Deputy Clyde Bucksteed, an attentive listener to the Ranger's story. "I was out with the ranchers when they went over the Bradded S range and we never saw hide nor hair of any stolen cattle."

"You just didn't know where to look," Danny explained. "There's a hidden valley, got good water and decent grazing in it. You can only get in through a tunnel at the back of a cave the ranchers probably never bothered to search. They'd figure the cattle couldn't be inside, I reckon, so they missed finding the hideout."

"How'd they get rid of the stolen stuff?" inquired the sheriff, showing interest for the first time.

"The agent at the Kaddo Reservation bought it from them. Got it at cheaper than the market price."

"You should have told me you was a Ranger," Simmonds complained. "Sounds like you didn't trust me."

"Figured I'd work better alone," Danny replied. "There's only one thing left to do now."

"What's that?" grunted Simmonds.

"Go to the Cattle Queen and pick up Soskice and Ed Wren."

A look of worry came to the sheriff's face. "I don't figure this's any of my fuss, Ranger. You come here without asking, played things as they suited you. Don't rightly see that I should tangle with a feller like Ed Wren just to please you."

"Won't come, huh?" asked Danny.

"Can't see my way to doing it," Simmonds replied.

"Then I'll take them alone."

Turning, Danny walked toward the office's front door. Clyde Bucksteed watched the Ranger and an admiring look came to his face. Slowly Clyde lifted his left hand to touch the badge he wore. In that moment Clyde Bucksteed changed from an office-filler, holding down his position because of his relationship with the sheriff, and became a man.

"I'm with you, Ranger," he said and followed Danny from the room.

Just as they stepped from the office, a man came racing his horse toward them. Seeing how excited the newcomer appeared to be, the two young lawmen halted and waited to see what caused the man's haste.

"I just found that pedlar, Jacobs. He's lying out

there 'bout a mile from town. Somebody shot him
in the back. From the look of his wagon, feller who
done it was after his money."

"How about it, Ranger?" Clyde asked.

"Let's go see Wren first. We might save ourselves
some work," Danny answered. "Jacobs sold me
out to Ella Watson, but he'd sold her to Cap'n
Murat first and I reckon she sent Wren after him."

"Best go see him then," said the deputy.

"Sure had," Danny agreed. "Let's go."

Before they had taken three steps along the
street, both saw the batwing doors of the saloon
open. Wren, Soskice and one of the bouncers
walked out, all wearing guns. While Soskice re-
mained standing on the sidewalk, Wren and the
bouncer stepped out, moving across the street.

"What're you wanting, Forgrave?" Soskice
called.

"You and Wren. We caught Stocker last night
and he told us everything."

"So now you plan to arrest me," the lawyer
went on.

"That's about the size of it," Danny said, not
breaking his stride.

"How about it, Mr. Wren?" asked the lawyer, a
sneer playing on his lips.

"He'll have to pass me first," Wren replied.

"My brother managed it easy enough that time
in Granite City," Danny said quietly, watching

Wren's face and leaving the handling of the bouncer to Clyde.

For an instant the confident sneer left Wren's face and he stared at the tall, blond young Ranger.

"Your brother?" croaked Wren and Danny detected a worried note in the hired killer's voice.

"My brother, Wren. My name's Danny Fog."

In that moment the scene came back before Wren's eyes. He was standing with the two men who hired him, looking at the Rocking H wagon and three cowhands who flanked·it. The small, blond man on the big paint stallion did most of the talking for the other side, winding up by saying, "Start the wagon, cookie."

"They's in the way, Cap'n," replied the cook reaching for the reins.

"Happen they'll move," Dusty Fog replied.

Well, the two fellers who hired Wren *had* moved, but the gunman could not without losing face. Instead he grabbed for his gun, meaning to down the small man. Only Dusty Fog did not look small any more. Suddenly he seemed to be the tallest of them all; and never had Wren seen such speed at drawing a gun. The Rio Hondo gun wizard's left hand flickered across his body and fetched out the Army Colt from his right holster even before Wren could clear his Remington. Wren remembered the sudden shock hitting him, the stunning knowledge that his speed failed to bring him through. Flame licked from Dusty Fog's gun and Wren's world dissolved first into red agony, then sank into black nothingness. When Wren recovered, he found he had lost a job and gained a bullet scar across the side of his head.

Now Dusty Fog's brother came toward Wren. Cold fear gripped the man, driving out the smug superiority which formed a gunfighting hard-case's best defense. Faced by Wren's look of expectancy and complete assurance that the gunman expected to be the one on his feet at the end of the affair, most men felt scared, unsure of themselves, hesitant and marked down as victims. Only this time Wren could not adopt the attitude as he studied the resemblance between the Fog brothers.

Uncertainty filled Wren. Maybe Danny Fog was not as fast as his brother. If so Wren ought to have a chance. If Danny Fog should be fast—Wren did not wish to think of the possibility. Yet Danny had not looked fast that first day. Of course, Fog would not have shown his true speed, knowing it might excite interest he wished to avoid in the performance of his Ranger chore. The thoughts ran through Wren's head as Danny and the deputy came closer, by the end of the saloon and halted not thirty feet away.

"Throw down your gun, Wren!" Danny ordered.

"Like hell!"

Letting the words out in a screech rather than a defiant snarl, Wren went for his gun. He beat Danny to the shot, but in his present nervous state the bullet missed the Ranger by inches. On the heels of Wren's shot, Danny got his right hand Colt out and working. Twice Danny fired, cocking the Colt on its recoil and slamming the two .44 bullets into Wren's chest. Danny shot the only way he dared under the circumstances, to kill. Knowing Wren to be faster, Danny did not dare give the man a chance to correct his aim. Caught by the bullets, Wren reeled backward. His gun fell from his hand as he crumpled to the ground.

Clyde Bucksteed had practiced fast drawing and shooting and now the training saved his life. Drawing, the deputy slammed a bullet into the bouncer an instant before the other threw down on him. Spinning around, the bouncer hit the hitching rail and hung on it yelling he was done.

Before leaving the saloon, Wren had sent the other bouncer through the side door to cover him. Coming down the alley between the saloon and the Wells Fargo office, the man stepped on to the street behind Danny and the deputy and brought up his gun. A rifle cracked further down the street and the bouncer—he had been the second of the hired guns reported by Jacobs to Murat—keeled over, a bullet in his head. Whirling to meet what might be a fresh menace, Danny and Clyde saw Simmonds standing outside his office, a smoking rifle in his hands.

"Watch Soskice!" yelled the sheriff, ambling forward.

Although he wore a gun, Soskice did not stand and fight. Instead he turned and flung himself back through the batwing doors, meaning to make his escape by the rear of the building. No sooner had the lawyer entered than a thud sounded and he shot out again, reeling backward across the sidewalk and crashing to the ground at Danny's feet.

Blowing on his knuckles, Izzy walked out of the building and looked down at the fallen lawyer. Having seen the way things went in the street, Izzy decided a change of sides might be to his advantage. So he prevented the lawyer's escape in an effort to prove his sterling regard for law and order.

His head spinning from the unexpected blow, Soskice looked up at the three lawmen as they gathered around him. Licking his lips nervously, he forced himself to his feet. Suddenly he no longer felt smug and superior to those humble, dull-witted fools who became peace officers because they lacked intelligence to do anything better with their lives.

"I—I want to help you!" Soskice whined. "I'll tell you enough to convict Ella Watson. It was her who sent Wren to kill that old pedlar."

Danny gave a look of disgust as he turned to the

sheriff. At least Ella Watson had refused to say anything either to avoid the blame or shift it on to somebody else.

"Take him to the jail, will you, Sheriff?" Danny said. "Hey what made you change your mind and cut in like that?"

"Got to figuring what Maw'd say if anything happened to Clyde and reckoned I didn't want it, her doting on the boy way she does. 'Sides, I might not be the best lawman in the world, but I reckoned the folks paid me for more than I'd been giving 'em. Let's go, Mr. Soskice, unless you know some law's says I can't take you down to the pokey."

Clearly Soskice could not think up a single law to avoid his arrest, for he went along with the sheriff in silence. Danny watched Clyde start some of the onlookers on cleaning up the street, then turned to the bartender.

"Is Mousey all right?" Danny asked.

"Got her a black eye and a few scratches and bruises, but nothing worse," Izzy replied. "She licked Dora good though, Phyl and Maisie stove each other up bad but the doctor tended to them. I wasn't in on anything, Ranger."

"I just bet you weren't," Danny said dryly. "Why'd Soskice and Wren stay on instead of running?"

"Miss Ella's got all the money in her safe and

they hoped she'd get back to give them travelling money. Is there anything I can do?"

"Sure, go back in there and hold the place until we come and see you."

Leaving Izzy to take care of the saloon, Danny walked along to the sheriff's office. There he and Simmonds interviewed the scared Soskice. At first the lawyer tried to lay all the blame on Ella Watson, but found he failed in his attempt to shift the blame.

"Us folks down in Texas might not be so full of high-minded ideas as fellers like you," Danny drawled. "So I'd surely hate to see what folks around here do to you when they hear that you've sold out your partner and tried to rail-road a *woman* to save your hide."

"They'll start reaching for a rope and looking for a tree," the sheriff went on.

Nor did Soskice doubt Simmonds's words. "Y—you'll protect me!" he whined, yet his tones lacked conviction. "It's your duty to protect me!"

"After the way you've belittled and mean-mouthed me all these months?" the sheriff replied. "You've dripped contempt over us lawmen all the time you've been here. So we'll be as useless as you reckon we are. If folks come a-lynching, me 'n' Clyde'll be long gone out of town."

"You—you won't let it happen, Ranger!" Soskice squeaked, turning to Danny.

"My work's done here," Danny answered. "I'll be riding real soon."

Raw fear glowed in Soskice's eyes. "W—would you protect me if I told you what brought me here? It's important to the peace of Texas."

"Try telling us," Danny said.

With the words pouring out in a flood, Soskice told all and laid bare a vicious scheme to wreck the flimsy peace of the Lone Star State. He belonged to Henry George's Socialist Party and was one of a group of college-educated intellectuals who wished to see Reconstruction continued until the Southerners they hated were smashed and the ex-slaves ruled the South. So some of their number came to Texas with the intention of stirring up so much trouble that the Federal Government brought back the old Reconstruction regime. In his fear for his life, Soskice named his friends and mentioned how the Sutton-Taylor feud and the Shelby County war had come about through the machinations of the intellectual bigots.

"Another range war going would have done it," Soskice finished, after telling how he helped Ella organize the cow stealing. "Not that I wanted things to go as far as that."

"Got to talking to Vic Crither the other day," drawled the sheriff. "He said as how it was you as first put the idea of hiring Gooch in his head."

"That's a lie!" yelped Soskice. "You can't prove it!"

"We'll try, *hombre*, we'll surely try," warned Danny. "Reckon you figured a killer like Gooch'd stir up fuss between the ranchers, especially if he downed the wrong men. It could have worked."

"It would have, if you hadn't happened along, Ranger," the sheriff put in. "I'm sure pleased I wrote for help."

And it proved later that Simmonds told the truth. He had written to Murat, but the letter went astray and did not arrive until days after Danny left for Caspar County. Nor was Simmonds as dishonest as Danny imagined. The sheriff's prosperity came from having sold his business, not from accepting bribes.

A telegraph message fetched in a judge and the heads of the Caspar County cow thieves were brought up for trial. Despite the killing of Gooch and Jacobs, Ella Watson received only five years in the penitentiary. Stocker did not intend to be alone in his punishment and so incriminated Soskice that they each drew ten years and might have counted themselves lucky to receive fifteen years each. Rangers swooped on the other members of Soskice's political gang and drove them out of Texas before they could make any more trouble.

"Well, that's the end of it, Calam, gal," Danny said as he and the girl rode side by side out of Caspar County. "It's a pity we couldn't stay on for Tommy and Mousey's wedding. At least the folks raised a collection that'll give them a good start, for Tommy's part in ending the cow stealing."

"Sure," agreed Calamity. "There's times I wonder what it'd be like to marry and settle down."

"Why not try it and see?"

"I'd never marry anybody who'd be fool enough to marry a gal like me," grinned Calamity. "Look at all the fun I'd miss. Say, I feel a mite sorry for Ella Watson. She was a dead game gal, even if her tracks ran crooked. And she gave me a danged good whirl. Wonder if she learned her lesson?"

Years later word reached Calamity of another cow stealing gang operating in Wyoming and following the Caspar County methods of using saloon-girls to ensnare the cowhands into the stealing. Then came news that the irate ranchers had caught and hung the man and woman involved. People called her Cattle Kate; but Calamity knew better, reckoning that Ella Watson had failed to change her ways and so met a cow thief's end.